FIRE TO THE FUSE

"We cannot?"

"Not tonight. Not right now."

"But, why not?" Matin drew away, looking up into Shell's eyes.

"There's something I have to do tonight. And it has to do with the safety of your people. I don't think you would want anything to stand in the way of that, would you, Matin?"

"No," she shook her head, "of course not—but what do you mean, Shelter Morgan? Do you mean you are taking the men out to fight tonight?"

"No. I'm going alone. I want to hit Realto again. I want to confuse and terrorize him."

There were plenty sticks of dynamite left in Shell's sack, and he planned to use every last one—almost. .. .

THE CONTINUING SHELTER SERIES
by Paul Ledd

#13: COMANCHERO BLOOD   (1208, $2.25)

A vengeance seeking U.S. Cavalry officer is on Shell's trail—and forcing him straight into a Comanchero camp of the meanest hombres in the West. The only soft spot is Lita, and the warm senorita's brother is the leader of the Comanchero outlaws!

#14: THE GOLDEN SHAFT   (1235, $2.25)

A captivating lady, who happens to own a gold mine, may be a lead to the man Shell's tracking. Before the gunsmoke clears, Shell has helped his lady friend save her mine, gets his man, and does a little digging in the shaft himself!

#15: SAVAGE NIGHT   (1272, $2.25)

Shell's leading a gang of down-and-dirty banditos into a trap—that holds a surprise for Shell as well! A savage chieftan's untamed daughter is about to welcome Shell south of the border!

#16: WITCHITA GUNMAN   (1299, $2.25)

Shelter's on the trail of an outlaw bandit who's leading him into Indian territory—where a savage buffalo hunter is keeping a woman as his slave, a woman *begging* to be rescued!

Available wherever paperbacks are sold, or order direct from the Publisher. Send cover price plus 50¢ per copy for mailing and handling to Zebra Books, 475 Park Avenue South, New York, N.Y. 10016. DO NOT SEND CASH.

#15

SHELTER

SAVAGE NIGHT
BY PAUL LEDD

ZEBRA BOOKS
KENSINGTON PUBLISHING CORP.

·ZEBRA BOOKS

are published by

KENSINGTON PUBLISHING CORP.
475 Park Avenue South
New York, N.Y. 10016

Printed in the United States of America

1.

The distant bugle was blowing reveille. Shelter Morgan opened his eyes and stared at the ceiling of the hotel room. Through the window faint gray dawn light bled. The strand of blond hair across Shelter's face tickled and he brushed it away.

He looked down appreciatively at the owner of the hair, seeing a peaceful sleeping face, a bare shoulder, the curve of breast, the swell of hips beneath the sheet. He rolled to Eveline and kissed her round, pink ear. Her eyelid fluttered and a slow, heavy yawn split her generous mouth.

"Whaiizit?"

"Wake up, Sarge. It's time to get back to the post."

"Noo," she complained, scooting nearer to Shell, throwing her long, sleek thigh over his leg.

"Yes. Come on now." She had burrowed in, her face buried against his chest, and now Shell rolled her onto her back, looking down into sleepy blue eyes.

"I don't want to, Shell. I want to stay here with you."

"Can't do it, Sarge. Remember what you said last night."

"I don't care about the colonel," she said, reaching up to pull his head down to her. She kissed his mouth with parted lips and Shelter felt Eveline shift, felt her legs part. The eyes were coming alert now, bright with expectation. She was warm and eager in the morning and Shelter found himself losing the argument.

"Sarge," he called her. Eveline James was the daughter of the post commander. Colonel Abel James was tall, square shouldered, and tough as nails. Iron gray hair clipped short, hard gray eyes and drooping gray mustache. He was tough enough to hold down Fort Sumner, New Mexico Territory against Apaches, Comancheros and bandit riff-raff, tough enough to keep his four hundred men walking the line.

And nearly tough enough to keep "Sarge" in line.

"Give me an hour," she purred, "and I'll go."

"If the colonel finds your bunk empty, Sarge, you're cooked. Remember what you told me—a fate worse than death: the finishing school in the East next time you're caught cutting up."

"One hour," she repeated, and there was no arguing with her.

Her hands slid down his thighs and across his hard buttocks then dipped between Shelter's legs, finding him ready. She gave a little pleasured sigh and positioned him, guiding him in with her fingers.

Her head lolled back and she gazed at him through half-closed, far away eyes as her hands ran up Shelter's spine and her hips began a slow, cadenced rolling.

Shelter kissed her breasts right and left, his tongue toying with her taut pink nipples. Eveline's body was trembling with need. Her legs lifted and wrapped around Shell, holding him near as her hips continued to sway and roll, as her pelvis nudged insistently against his.

She was clutching at his back, her teeth nipping at his shoulder and chest and Shell began to thrust deeply,

6

feeling her moist warmth, the slight clutching of her inner muscles as she rocked against him spreading her legs until they could spread no more.

Eveline began to mutter small indistinct words, to claw at Morgan. She bit down hard on her lip, her head rolling from side to side as Shell buried himself to the hilt.

Eveline gasped with pleasured surprise, went rigid and suddenly came completely undone. Her body bucked and pitched, her hands dug between Shell's legs, grasping his sack, pulling him closer as her body flooded with fluid. She was whispering into Shelter's ear now, her breath warm and moist, urging him on, her hands touching him where he entered her and Shelter reached a sudden hard climax.

She lay back, her hand still holding him, feeling the slow pulsing. Shelter lay on top of her still, nestled between her breasts, his thudding heartbeat slowing.

The sunlight through the window was warm on his back and he drifted off to sleep again.

It was then that the dream came again. Shelter was back in Georgia, along the bloody Conasauga River. There was gold scattered across the ground and gunsmoke filling the clearing. A bullet smashed into Welton Williams who sat his horse next to Morgan and Williams was blown from the saddle, his blood spraying Morgan's hand and arm. Shell saw Thornton go down, saw the Dink get hit, felt the scalding impact of a bullet.

And the gold. The gold lay there scattered across the ground, spattered with blood as the guns roared.

Shelter woke up with a start. He was bathed in sweat.

"What's wrong?" Sarge asked. She was sitting over him, forming a lovely picture in the morning light. Her golden hair flowed across her shoulders, her blue eyes

7

sparkled. There was concern on her beautiful mouth.

"Nothing. A nightmare," Shell said, rubbing his face as he sat up, putting his feet on the floor. Sarge hugged him briefly, her breasts against his back warm and soft.

"I've got to get going," she said, bouncing from the bed. Shelter only nodded.

He sat watching her dress, slipping into a chemise, tugging it down over her hips, smiling coyly, knowing that she was inflaming him again. Shelter turned his thoughts away—or tried to. The sun was an hour old now. At Fort Sumner, Col. Abel James had been up for a long while. And he had already undoubtedly discovered that Eveline had not slept home last night.

"I can get out of it," Eveline said, reading his thoughts.

"Sure."

"Don't worry about a thing," she said brightly. She stood, pinning her hair up hastily. "I'll tell him I went riding early—some such thing."

Shelter walked to her and put his hands around her waist. She placed her hands over his and leaned back against him. "All right," he said, kissing her neck just below the ear before stepping back, "you'd better get going."

"Tonight?" she asked hopefully, turning toward him.

"I don't know."

"Say we can," she urged him, her hand resting on his thigh.

"We can. Now get!"

She kissed him quickly and went to the door of the hotel room. Peering out she turned to give Shelter a little wave and then she was gone, closing the door softly behind her. Shelter walked to the window and looked out

8

at the empty streets of the town, standing naked in the warm sunlight for a long minute before, with a shrug, he walked to where his clothes lay in a jumble on the floor.

He dressed and went downstairs to breakfast, sitting alone in the corner of the restaurant dining room. He had eggs and potatoes and ham with a quart of coffee. He was just finishing his last cup when the soldiers came in through the front door.

There were four of them, a big chested sergeant leading them. His eyes scanned the room, settled on Morgan and flickered meaningfully. The soldier hitched up his pants and said something to his men. They crossed the room purposefully toward Morgan's table.

"You Shelter Morgan?" he asked, hovering over the tall, lean, blue-eyed man.

"That's right."

"Grab your hat. Colonel James wants to see you."

So Sarge hadn't made it back. Morgan shook his head. "Suppose I don't want to go?"

"Then we'll take you the hard way."

"Does this look like a blue uniform I'm wearing, Sergeant?"

"Yes, sir," he answered with a crooked little smile, "it does to me. You look exactly like a man who's gone AWOL. How's that strike you?"

"I'll come along," Shelter said, there wasn't much choice. There were four of them and they looked willing if not eager to do it the hard way. He snatched up his hat, left two dollars for the waitress and rose.

They walked together to the hotel door and out into the brilliant warm sunshine. It was dry and dusty outside. A light westerly wind picked up the dust along the main street and drifted it. Ahead of Morgan was the dark,

9

stocky form of Fort Sumner, and beyond it dung colored mountains.

He walked slowly toward the post, the sergeant behind him, nudging him mentally, the soldiers following. They went in through a side gate and on across the parade ground where soldiers drilled.

"The colonel's office is that way, Morgan," the big man said and Shelter turned toward it.

The soldiers remained outside as Shelter and the NCO entered the long, low log building. "Wait here a minute," the sergeant said. Then he went in through an inner door. In a moment he was back, beckoning. Shelter took a deep breath and went on in.

The colonel sat behind his desk, iron hard, capable and all business. He nodded toward a wooden chair and Shell took it.

"Shelter Morgan?"

"That's right."

"I've been looking for you."

"Have you? Why?"

The colonel didn't answer. The colonel wasn't used to answering questions. He gave orders and they were obeyed. That was it.

"We want to talk to you. If you'll wait just a minute." The colonel rose and strode toward the door. Shelter heard him asking for someone. Eveline no doubt. Or her mother. Maybe the sheriff.

Five minutes later a man arrived, however. He looked at Morgan and grunted. Tall, narrow eyed, blond, the man wore a gray town suit and white hat.

"What's going on here, exactly?" Morgan asked. He was leaning back in his chair comfortably, hat on his knee.

"It will all become clear shortly, Morgan. If you'll just be patient."

"All right." Shelter had some patience. He had developed it highly during the seven years he spent in a Federal prison at war's end.

"This is Mister Reese. He's come down from the capital hoping to find you."

"Call me Jack," Reese said, and he smiled. There was good humor in that smile, but there was something strained in the eyes, some burden the man was carrying.

"All right, Jack. Suppose we get on with this."

"Do you mind if I ask you a few questions?"

"Go ahead."

"Shelter Morgan, formerly a captain in the Confederate army. Arrested on spy charges at the end of the war."

"That's me."

"But you weren't a spy, were you?"

"No." Shelter decided to give it to them straight. What was going on here he couldn't guess, but he didn't think it would be to his advantage to try being cute. They probably already knew anyway. "I had crossed over the lines and I was wearing civilian clothes when they caught me, but I wasn't a spy."

"What were you doing?" Jack Reese asked, sitting on the corner of the colonel's desk.

"I think you know, but I'll tell you. I was ordered to go across the lines and make my way toward Lookout Mountain. During the battle for Chickamauga a man named General Custis had hidden some Confederate property there."

"Property?"

"Gold. A quarter of a million dollars in gold. I went

11

across under the cover of night, sticking to the high ridges, the back trails."

"You knew the country?"

"I was born not far from Lookout. That's why they chose me."

"You recovered the gold."

"Yes. We had some luck. I lost one man who was told to keep his head down and didn't, but we recovered the gold which was to be used for medical supplies, for food and blankets, for shoes. At least that was what I was told. And we needed those items, Reese, needed them badly. There were men dying in horrible pain, men freezing to death, men whose feet were going to have to be amputated because they had frostbite from walking barefoot through the snow to fight. That's how bad it was by that time."

"The gold, I take it," the colonel put in, "did not get to where it was going."

Shelter's eyes narrowed, his gaze sharpened as he looked at Abel James. "No," he said, "it never got to where it was going and as a result hundreds of men died that winter."

"What happened?" Reese asked.

"There were four of us escorting the gold back to Georgia. We were elated. We had beaten the odds and made it back carrying that gold. A man had ridden out to meet us and he led us to where General Custis and Colonel Fainer, my commanding officer were waiting. They weren't alone.

"There were twenty men there sitting their horses in a clearing. Twenty of them, officers and men. All of them were in civilian clothes."

"You knew what they wanted."

12

"Yes," Shelter said, "I knew right away. There was a lot of talk about the war being over, about us taking what we could get and getting the hell out of there. The general was talking like that, saying that anyone but a fool knew the war was lost, that something was owed to us . . . then the guns started firing. I still don't know who started it, but suddenly there were guns shooting at us from all directions. When it was over they had the gold and I was the only one left behind alive to tell about it."

"Did you talk about it?" the colonel asked with genuine interest, it seemed.

"Yes, Colonel, I did. At first. I went to the Justice Department but they just weren't interested. The war had been over for a long time. The men involved were scattered across the country, most of them coming West. I was told that it was impossible to find all of them, that they were probably living under assumed names, that the entire West couldn't be combed for these men. If they had been found, if the government had put years of effort and thousands of dollars into the job, well, I was told, there still wasn't any case. It was my word against theirs, and that just doesn't carry any legal weight."

"So you took things into your own hands."

"That's right." Shelter's lips compressed into a fine line. "I took it into my own hands."

Jack Reese and Colonel James exchanged a quick glance. It was Reese who spoke.

"Morgan, do you know a man named Zachary Willits?"

"Yes," Shelter said, his eyes going cold and hard.

"He was one of them, wasn't he?"

"He was one of them. Master Sergeant Zack Willits. He's a murdering thief."

13

"You're right there," the colonel muttered.

"Have you got him?" Shelter asked. "Or do you know where he is? What exactly is it you men want from me? I've answered all of your questions; now I think it's time you answered some of mine."

"Yes," Jack Reese agreed, "I think it is time we answered you. Colonel?"

The colonel nodded. He walked to a filing cabinet, opened the top drawer and removed a bottle of whisky. He poured out a glass for himself and for Reese. Shelter declined.

"We want Willits," the colonel said, settling behind his desk. "We want him badly—but we can't touch him."

"Why so?"

"He's out of the country. Let me sketch in the background for you. Willits as you may or may not know has three brothers. All of them alike facially—like a row of whisky jugs sitting on a shelf. Heavy in the body, heavy in the face."

"Big and ugly."

"True. Big and ugly and peculiarly nasty. They came west together after the war and started poking around for a way to make a living. Almost everything they found took hard work and plenty of it. They were working cattle for a local brand when Ben Willits got into a saloon fight and killed a man. They all took off together. Since they were on the run anyway, they decided to make it fun. They held up a bank in Riverton, killed a clerk and set half the town afire.

"They went into Mexico to elude the law and down there they apparently made contact with a man named Hector Villa."

"Villa's game is revolution," Reese put in. "He's been

14

raising hell down south with his army of peasants and bandits. Blew up the armory in Durango last year, tried to assassinate the Agriculture Secretary in Mexico City."

"What did he want from the Willits brothers?" Shelter asked. "Zachary Willits couldn't hold a thought long enough to bring something like that off."

"I'll tell you exactly what he wanted. We know now because he got it. Fifteen hundred rifles, twelve-thousand rounds of ammunition and two gatling guns. The Willits boys hit an army train six miles from here. They killed every single man aboard. Twenty-three people, Morgan, and made off with the weapons."

"There was some payroll money and a half dozen cases of dynamite as well," the colonel added.

"You know it was Willits?" Shell asked, his eyes growing intent.

"I do—I said they killed all the men with that wagon train, and they did. One of them lived long enough to tell us who had done it, however."

"Now they're in Mexico. Where?"

The colonel looked at Reese who cleared his throat and told Morgan, "According to a contact we have cultivated in Mexico, Villa and the Willits brothers are in a place called Escebar, that's near Tampico on the Gulf Coast."

"But you can't touch them."

"No. Relations are a bit strained with the Mexican government right now. They're not going to allow any American army forces to cross over. Nor, unfortunately, do they have the strength to do the job. Escebar is a long way from Mexico City, a long way from any army post of any size. And Villa has a large force, he has weapons now—and good ones, those fifteen hundred rifles were repeating Winchesters. Did you know that most of the

Mexican army is still carrying muzzle loaders? They wouldn't have a chance before Villa. He's set up his own little kingdom in Escebar, and damn me if it doesn't look as if he'll be able to hold it."

Shelter recrossed his legs. He looked thoughtfully at the colonel and then at Reese.

"We want you to go down there, Morgan."

"Alone?"

"Nearly alone."

"Against an army and their gatling guns."

"Yes. Damnit, Morgan, they killed twenty-three soldiers! How many men died during the war because of what Willits and the others did when they snatched that gold?"

"Hundreds, sir. There's no accounting, and three good friends of mine before my eyes."

"Then . . ."

"Still—it's impossible, isn't it? What you're asking makes no sense. Go down there and pull the Willits brothers out from under Villa's nose."

"Yes," Colonel James said, "it's impossible or as near to it as makes no difference."

Shelter nodded. "When do I start?"

2.

"The only plan we could come up with has you drifting in to Escebar representing yourself as a mercenary. Villa should be interested. He's got plenty of men, not too many skilled soldiers. I'd like you to familiarize yourself with the gatling gun before you leave."

"Not necessary," Shell said.

"You've used one?"

"Yes." Shelter put what was a very unpleasant memory aside. Changing subjects he said, "You told me I'd be 'nearly alone' on this job. What did you mean?"

It was Reese who answered. "We've gotten this much cooperation from the Mexican government—they informed us that they have an agent in place, a member of Villa's band who's feeding back information. It's where the idea for sending you in came from," the government man admitted.

"All right. What's his name?"

"Madrid. The Mexican government is especially anxious that you don't uncover this agent, Morgan."

"That's not what I'm going there for," Shell replied. What was he going there for? It was a madman's mission. He had begun to wonder about himself. This hatred which could not be suppressed, this need to mete out the justice these men had eluded. A need to bring order into

17

the cosmos at the cost of his own safety. Maybe, and it had been suggested by others, he had lost touch with reality somewhere. Along the bloody Conasauga River, perhaps, or during those years sitting alone in a stony, cold cell staring at a small, empty window.

"I don't know what you'll do about being recognized. I wouldn't shave for a while if I were you. Maybe you can come up with some other sort of disguise."

"It's only Zack Willits that could recognize me, and it's been a long while now. Of course it could be that Villa isn't interested in hiring any Yankee soldiers just now."

"It could be, but he needs leaders—at least that's the assessment of the Mexican agent in place. Madrid says the man's got nothing but a rabble army. He enforces discipline via the death penalty—he has to."

"Sounds lovely," Shelter said. "When do I leave?"

"As soon as possible. I'll let you have whatever supplies you want. Horses, ammunition, food."

"Morgan?" Reese spoke again as Morgan rose and pulled on his hat. "You know there's many times the army, the government can't legally arrest or pursue criminals. The Willits case is only one example. They're bloody killers, scum, yet we can't touch them because they've gone over some imaginary line in the desert. It's like a child's game—you can't touch me because I'm on home base—but the losers in this game die."

"What are you trying to tell me?"

"Just this, they know who you are in Washington. They know what you've been doing and know that you're peculiarly effective at it."

"It's also very probably illegal."

"Yes, and so are many other things that are right and necessary. There are occasions when even the govern-

18

ment has to proceed in an extra-legal fashion to do what is necessary. Maybe there's a place for a man with your talents. It's possible that there are other services you could perform for the government, one day when you've done with what you have to do. They asked me to tell you that."

"I'll remember it," Shelter said. He shook Reese's hand and the colonel's and started toward the door. James spoke as his hand touched the doorknob.

"There's really no need to say goodbye to my daughter, Morgan."

Shelter grinned without turning around. "No, sir," he said soberly. Then he went out into the orderly room and on outside to stand on the plankwalk for a minute, glancing at the high sky. Then, his expression growing grim, he stepped down and started walking back toward town.

Shell settled his hotel bill, got his gray horse out of the stable and returned to the fort. By that time the word had been passed to the sutler that Morgan was to be given whatever he asked for in the way of supplies, courtesy of Colonel James.

Shelter loaded up on tinned goods, flour, coffee and sugar, throwing in an extra Colt .44 and a spare bowie which he tucked in his bedroll. After that he walked to the paddock and selected a pack horse from the army stock. Half an hour later he was out onto the desert, riding away from Fort Sumner and toward Mexico. His eyes and thoughts on the rough land ahead of him.

He didn't much like the odds in this one, but he wanted Willits. He wanted him badly. He could still see the big man sitting his horse, a smirk on his wide, ugly face. He could still see Willits firing his pistol into Welton

Williams' body.

Why, he wondered, did Willits have to ride for a man like Villa? Willits' cut of the gold should have been enough to allow him to live differently. But then maybe Willits craved the violence. He wanted to kill.

Shelter looked around him at the changing land. He was into red sand country now. Several low mesas bulked against the skyline to the south. Nothing grew on the desert but crimson-tipped ocotillo and nopal cactus. There would be little else for hundreds of miles.

Escebar was different entirely. It was down on the coast where ancient, very advanced civilizations had flourished for a time, building strange pyramids and temples in the jungle. Nothing lasted long down there. The jungle grew back faster than man could cut it down. Villa had chosen well. Escebar was remote and nearly inaccessible. The government didn't want control badly enough to contest Villa in that jungle, and so for the time being he was the emperor of that corner of the world.

The days dragged past, mile after dusty mile with the sun beating down on Shell's back, the horse trudging forward, head bowed low. It was on the sixth day out of Sumner that he came upon the bandits.

There were three of them, crouched around another figure in the sundown-painted wash. Morgan held up, dropping the lead rope to his pack horse.

They had someone down. Down or dead, and they were rifling his pockets.

"None of your business, Morgan," he told himself. But by then he had already drawn his rifle from its boot and, nudging the gray with his knees he was silently approaching the three bandits.

A head came around and Shelter heard the man cry out

20

a warning. The bandit went for his holstered gun and Shell cut loose. The .44-40 bullet slammed into the first bandit's chest and he was punched back to sprawl against the sand, dead.

The others sprinted for their horses, firing as they ran, and Shelter let them go. They were mounted and riding hard to the west minutes later, Shell's warning shots singing over their heads.

He waited until he could not see the bandits anymore, until the sun was a dully glowing red ball above the dark western hills, then he rode down into the wash.

He checked the bandit first. Dead, as Morgan had expected. Their victim lay unmoving against the sand, one leg tucked up under his body.

He was only a kid, seventeen or eighteen. A trickle of blood ran from the corner of his mouth and he had a lump on his forehead, but he was alive and apparently not badly injured.

Shelter walked to his horse, getting his canteen. He also took the eye patch from his saddlebags. He had decided to wear it along with a growth of beard to disguise himself once he had reached Escebar. Now seemed as good a time as any to start wearing it.

He walked back to where the kid lay, got down to one knee and lifted his head, pouring a few drops of water onto his lips. The kid's tongue flicked out in an unconscious response. Shelter poured a little more water and again he drank.

One eye opened slowly and Shell saw fear in it as he looked at Morgan.

"Who're you? Where are they?"

"They're gone." Two of them anyway. "I saw them working you over."

21

The conversation had been in Spanish up to this point, now the kid, noticing that his savior was an American, shifted over to passable English.

"I didn't even see them come. They just knocked me down while I was tending to my horse. It had cut its hoof on a rock. Where is my horse?" He looked around frantically and tried to get up.

"Looks like it's gone. You all right? Can you sit up?"

"Yes." He made it to a sitting position and Shell gave him the canteen. "I am Armando Sandoval. You may call me Mando, okay?"

"All right. I'm Jim Pike," Morgan said.

"I thank you, Jim Pike. They would have killed me I think."

"Did you know them?"

"No. They were nothing. Just Indio bandits."

"I'm going on up to the top of the rise and take a last look around before the sun goes down," Shell told him, "then I'll be back to break out some food. You hungry?"

"Yes." He smiled sheepishly. "I have not eaten for two days."

Morgan picked up his rifle and walked up the sandy slope to the rise. There he stood peering into the dying sun, searching the land. The bandits were gone. Returning to the camp he found Mando on his feet. He wavered a bit, but the color was returning to his face.

"Did you see my horse?"

"Not a sign of him."

Mando sighed. "Now what, I wonder?"

"You said you haven't eaten for a couple of days. You're a long way from home then."

"Too far to walk—if I was going home, but I'm not. Never again. There is nothing in our village. Nothing at all."

"Where were you going?" Shell asked. He had crouched down to open a tin of beef with his knife. Mando watched him, studying the bearded, one-eyed American for a minute before he answered.

"I am going to fight the war."

"What war?"

"The war against oppression," Mando said passionately.

"Sounds like a good war if you've gotta fight a war," Morgan replied.

"Do not mock me, Jim Pike."

"I'm not, kid. Here, have some of this meat." He handed the can to Mando who took it hesitantly but ate it greedily, his dark eyes flashing at Morgan.

"Where's this war being fought exactly?" Shelter asked, crouching down to eat with his knife.

"Escebar," Mando said excitedly, crouching down to face Morgan. Shelter felt his mouth tighten.

"Where's that?" he asked.

"Not far. Perhaps another hundred miles. Hector Villa is there they say!"

"Who?" Shell asked disinterestedly.

"*Who?*" Mando repeated in disbelief. "Hector Villa, the greatest man in all of Mexico, he who stand up for the rights of the oppressed people and fights the tyranny of the government."

"Oh." Shell tossed his empty tin can aside and drank from the canteen, washing the salty taste away. Mando was still looking at him as if he'd come down from another planet.

"Haven't you heard of Hector Villa?"

"I believe I have," Shell said.

23

"That is where I am going—or was going. Now I do not know. Without a horse . . ." he spread his hands.

"You're a soldier, are you?" Shell asked with a smile.

"Yes," Mando said with pride. "Well, not yet. But I will be. Once I learn how."

"What's it pay?" Morgan asked. "Or does it?"

"Yes, there will be pay, but I do not care for that. Only for the war of liberation."

"That's all Villa cares about too, I guess," Shelter said. "Of course."

"Well, that's fine to have those high-minded ideals, I guess, but me, I'd only do something like that for the pay, for a lot of pay."

"You are a soldier too?" Mando asked cautiously.

"I have been." Shelter had made his bed and now he stretched out on it, looking at the stars.

"Maybe now you need work," Mando suggested.

"Maybe."

"Maybe you would travel south with me and join the army of Hector Villa."

"I don't know about that, Mando. I meant what I said about the pay, it would have to be pretty good."

"You could talk to them! You could ask what they would pay you."

"Maybe. I was sort of thinking of taking it easy for a while. We'll see, Mando. We'll see in the morning, all right?"

"Yes. In the morning," the kid said, obviously excited.

Morgan slept with one eye open, half expecting Mando to try taking off with his horses in the middle of the night, but it didn't happen.

They rose early while it was still cool and had another meal out of tin cans. Mando watched Morgan expectantly all through breakfast. Finally he blurted out, "Well? What have you decided?"

"About what?" Shelter asked, yawning.

"About taking me south, about us joining the army of Hector Villa, Jim."

"That. Look, Mando, are you sure you want to do this. It'll be a rough life. Besides, maybe things aren't as you imagine them to be."

"What do you mean?"

"I mean this war may be different than what you've been told. Maybe Hector Villa won't be what you think he is."

"Of course he will be," Mando said with confidence. He was very young, Shelter decided. "You will see. We agree? You will go with me and fight."

"Yes," Shelter said after a minute, "I'll go with you. We'll fight. If the pay is right," he added.

"After you have met Hector Villa, after he has explained to you what this war is about, you will refuse your pay," Mando said.

They rode south slowly, Mando singing as they rode. The land began to change. The air was humid, and in the distance Shell could see mountains, their flanks overgrown by jungle. There was grass now, knee high to a horse, and water, much of it stagnant, pooled in marshy bogs.

"Now we must ride carefully," Mando told Morgan and Shell gave him a questioning glance. "Ahead," he lifted his chin toward the mountain jungles, "is the land of the Tamaulipas."

"What's that?"

"Indians, Jim, very savage Indians, their lives no different than they were a thousand years ago. The

25

Spanish tried to uproot them, but the jungle defeated them. The jungle and the ferocity of the Tamaulipas."

By late afternoon they were into the jungle itself. Mando was no longer singing his songs. His dark eyes darted from place to place nervously. Shelter couldn't blame him, but he was awful nervous for a man who wants to make warfare a way of life.

Twice Morgan saw them. Twice silent shadows, blurs against the background of forest and jungle. Runners. Tamaulipas taking the word to their village that two strangers were riding through their mysterious and ancient land.

They camped without a fire that night. Shell slept sitting up, propped against a fallen tree, pistol in his hand. Parrots had shrieked in the jungle all day long and now the night birds began. Once Morgan heard the chilling roar of a jaguar far distant, and later another indefinable, bloody sound which might have been a woman wailing with grief or a man screaming at the moment of death.

When they awoke in the morning Mando looked as if he hadn't had a moment's rest. His eyes were ringed darkly. He didn't look so young as he had the day before.

"Look," he said shakily. He was pointing at their supplies and Morgan, walking nearer, looked down and frowned. Half of their gear was missing. There were footprints around their packs, the bare prints of an Indian. He had come in, gone through their gear, taken what he wanted and departed again, all without making enough sound to alert Morgan who was a very light sleeper. If he had wanted to, he could easily have slit their throats while he was at it.

26

"Let's get moving," Shelter said, and Mando started packing eagerly. He didn't like this place and Morgan didn't blame him a bit.

When they were on the trail again, Shell asked him, "You sure you know where we're going, Mando?"

"Oh, yes. I have not been here before but I asked the old man, Pablo, who used to live in Escebar. He said to find the river and then follow it to the coast. We cannot go wrong."

Or so he hoped. They rode slowly through the rain forest. Above them huge trees canopied the earth, nearly blocking out the sunlight which was diffused, shining like golden droplets through the interwoven boughs.

The trees were hung with vines and sometimes with snakes, slithering around and up the trees, hanging in green loops, their glittering little eyes alert for any opportunity. They saw a family of coatimundi cross the trail ahead of them. Small, harmless animals looking like stretched out raccoons. In lots of places they were kept for pets.

Shell felt the slight impact on the skirt of his saddle and was already reacting before he had glanced down to see the slender dart which was imbedded there. He slid to the off-side of his horse, hissing to Mando who looked back with terror and did the same. Shell had his Colt in his hand, but no target presented itself. There was nothing, absolutely nothing but the dense, deep green jungle, the orange and metallic green flash of a parrot settling in a tree.

Half a mile on they stopped to examine the saddle.

"Poison," Mando said as Shelter pulled the dart cautiously from the saddle leather. It was a nasty looking

27

little thing, barbed, the tip of it smeared with some dark, gummy substance—very likely poison as Mando suggested.

"What do you think, Jim?" the kid asked, his eyes wide and not at all warriorlike.

"I think we'd better keep moving," Shelter said. "That may have been just a warning. I've got the feeling that if the man who shot this dart had wanted to hit me, he would have."

"Yes," Mando agreed readily, "we shall keep moving."

Out of the jungle of the Tamaulipas Indians and into the jungle of Hector Villa.

They found the river two hours later, a slow-rolling wide and shallow river winding through the jungle toward the coast. It wasn't possible to ride along the banks of the river, but they kept it in sight through the trees as they headed east toward the coast.

It was dusk when they emerged onto a broad plain. The sky was a hazy purple, yet it seemed bright after the hours in the murky jungle. Below them was a jumble of white buildings with red roofs. Farther yet was the Gulf, glittering a deep blue in the late sunlight. The coastline curved slowly away, a narrow white beach faded to dull red marking the coastline.

Mando was beside Shelter as he halted his horse to look over the land. The kid was cheerful again, flushed with excitement as they sat above the little coastal town.

"Escebar," he said. "Our difficulties are over, Jim."

Or just beginning, depending on how you look at it. Escebar. Hector Villa, the Willits brothers were waiting down there and Shelter had felt more comfortable, more secure in the jungle with the roving Indians than he did now as he looked at the town of Escebar.

28

"Let's have at it," he said, and Mando looked at his friend, the one-eyed Jim Pike, wondering at the tone of his voice. The tall man's mouth was set grimly, his eye was cold and steely. An uneasy premonition flitted through Mando's mind, but it passed quickly away, and with Jim Pike beside him he started down the long slopes toward the peaceful-appearing village below.

Ahead lay Mando's dreams of glory and valor, his idol, Hector Villa, adventure and romance—and more blood than Mando Sandoval could begin to imagine.

3.

It was full dark when they rode up the main street of Escebar, their horses' hoofs clattering on the cobbles. There were lights on in most windows, and the sound of guitar playing from a cantina they passed. A young, beautiful girl with flashing dark eyes was brushing her long raven black hair on an overhanging balcony and she gave Shelter a curious and haughty glance.

They could smell the salt of the sea in the air, and the enticing smells of spicy food being cooked. That was the first order of business—eating, and Shelter kept his eyes open for a restaurant. They found one three blocks on where the avenue widened into a round plaza. They had planted grass there, and around the fountain which splashed away in the center of the plaza, there were bright red poinsettias.

There were half a dozen horses tied up at the rail outside of the restaurant when Morgan swung down from the gray, loosened the cinches and led the way inside.

Mando stood beside the door, hat in hand as they entered. Shell let his gaze sweep the room. There were six tough-looking men, half of them wearing beards, at a large round table in a back corner. The table was mounded with tamales and enchiladas. Three pitchers of

30

cerveza sat around the food. Dark eyes came up to glance at Shelter Morgan then returned to the food and beer.

"There is a table," Mando said, nodding to one just inside the door and Morgan followed him to it. "I am afraid," the kid said as they sat down, "that I have no money with me, Jim."

"I'll pick it up this time," Shelter said, and Mando grinned with relief. He eyed the waitress walking past with plates of steaming food eagerly, fidgeting in his chair until they had ordered.

Shelter glanced around again while waiting to be served. At the table in the back the six Mexicans continued to attack the mountain of food before them, calling periodically for more beer.

"Villa's men?" Shelter asked, and Mando's eyes too shifted to the back table.

"I think so, don't you?"

"Yes." They looked the part. Savage, dirty, with dull, cunning little eyes. They wore bandoliers crossed over their chests. Weapons stuck out everywhere, pistols and knives, a machete or two. Behind them, leaning against the wall were half a dozen new, but not well cared for Winchester repeaters, probably those stolen from the army in New Mexico.

Their food came and Shelter pulled his elbows off the table while the hot platters were placed down.

"Cerveza?" the heavy waitress asked.

"Please."

She waddled away, returning in minutes with a pitcher of icy beer. Shell was already eating. Mando was going after it as if he was afraid it would run away. Shell smiled, feeling momentarily sorry for the kid. Living in a poverty-ridden town with no prospects of improving himself he had developed some kind of romantic notion about Villa and decided to become a bandido himself.

He couldn't know what he was getting into. Shelter did—he had seen the Villas of this world before, seen their cruelty, their viciousness. He hadn't yet seen one who delivered what he promised the gullible—social reform, wealth, dignity. Usually things only got worse.

The kid was going to be bitterly disillusioned, but just now everything was bright and wonderful in his world. His eyes were closed to any suggestion of evil. Shelter Morgan was going in with his eyes wide open. He wasn't sure which of them was the bigger fool.

They were still eating when the Mexicans at the back table rose noisily, their chairs scraping the floor, and with much shouting and clattering picked up their weapons and tramped across the floor toward the front door of the restaurant.

"Do you want to speak to them, Jim?" Mando asked, leaning forward.

"No."

"They may be able to tell us where Villa is."

"We'll find him, don't worry."

Shelter kept his eyes on his plate, all the same he knew that Villa's soldiers were looking at him as they passed out of the restaurant. Mando's face was almost worshipful. He wanted to follow along after them.

"Eat," Morgan told him, "we'll find Villa and you'll get your gun."

They finished up and Shelter sat there sipping his beer for another ten minutes. The kid was so impatient to be going that Shell drank the last of his beer faster than he

32

wanted to. Then they rose, Morgan leaving some silver money on the table to pay for their meal.

They were waiting outside when Shelter and Mando came out of the restaurant.

Six men standing and crouched around Shell's horse. They had his pack off, his saddlebags unstrapped. One of them hissed as Morgan stepped out onto the plankwalk, Mando at his shoulder, and their faces turned toward Shell.

"What is happening?" Mando squeaked.

A man laughed. "We are from the customs inspector. We saw a *Norte Americano* and so we must search his things to see what he has brought into Mexico."

It wasn't very funny, but it got a big laugh from his compadres. Morgan looked at them silently. They had their rifles in their hands and their look was challenging, but not expectant. They didn't anticipate this one man going against them. They should have.

"Pick it all up again and tie it back where you found it," Shelter said, his voice soft, but with a chilling edge to it. "And do it neatly."

A man laughed hoarsely. "Oh, yes, anything you say, mister! Who you think you are, mister?"

"I'm the man who owns those things," Shell said, his voice still soft, quietly menacing. Reaching behind him he took Mando's arm and shoved the kid aside, out of the possible line of fire.

"Are you crazy! Don't you know us? We are Hector Villa's men. I am Gato Hernandez."

"We've all got troubles," Shell said dryly. The big man stiffened and he started to bring his rifle around before Shell, stepping nearer, said, "I wouldn't do that, Gato."

33

It was then that Hernandez noticed the gun in the stranger's hand. How it had gotten there, Gato did not know. He only knew that it was leveled at his fat belly and that the hammer of the pistol was drawn back, the finger of the American on the curved trigger.

"There are six of us," Gato blustered. He looked around as if to assure himself there were still five men with him.

"Six of you to pick up my goods and tie them back on my horse," Shelter said.

"You think you will kill us all!"

"I think I'll kill one fat Gato if they don't start putting those things away," Shelter said with a peculiarly nasty little smile which did nothing for Gato's confidence.

Hernandez seemed to waver for a moment. Pride demanded that he order his men to shoot, that he try to bring his own rifle up and fire, but Hernandez was not that stupid. He liked his life, cherished his body. Was it worth it? Over a few trinkets?

"Pack his things up again," Gato said with a snarl.

"Tell them to do it neatly," Shell said, pressing it.

Gato gurgled with anger, but he swallowed his argument. "Do it neatly," he said, bringing a snicker from one of his own men.

"We will meet again," Hernandez said.

"You're right, we will. I'm going to be your new boss, Hernandez."

"You are what? Did Villa send for you?" he asked, suddenly shaken.

"No. But I'll be along all the same. I heard Villa needs some help teaching his people how to be soldiers. Tonight I've found out what they mean. We'll meet again, but

34

don't try anything when we do, Gato. I don't get any nicer than I have been tonight." Then again he smiled that humorless smile and Gato, frowning, turned away and walked silently toward his horse.

Shelter watched them mount up, watched them ride away across the plaza. Then he holstered his gun and let out a deep slow breath.

"Jim!" Mando was visibly shaken. "What were you doing? You could have been killed!"

"That's right," Shelter said. "From here on it's possible at all times. And the same holds for you, Mando. Where we're going guns are a way of life, death is commonplace. If you'll listen to me you'll turn around right now and ride home. You're not cut out for this, my friend."

"Go home? How can I go home after all I have told the people there? Besides," he said, bracing himself, "I am brave. I will prove it. I just didn't want to see you hurt, Jim, you are a friend of mine."

"All right, friend, let's get on down the road then. I mean to be in Villa's camp tonight."

"After this," Mando said as he swung aboard his horse, "will we be welcome?"

"Doesn't matter much if I'm welcome or not, I'm going. It doesn't mean you have to go though, Mando. Last chance to change your mind."

The kid just shook his head and so Shelter, his saddle cinched up, swung aboard the gray and turned it northward across the plaza, riding in the direction Gato Hernandez and his men had taken.

There wasn't much to following them. There was only one road out of town, and their dust still hung heavily in

35

the air. The moon had begun to rise over the Gulf and now Morgan could see that the trail led down toward the beach, following it northward. There was a low, dark promontory ahead of them, and situated on the high ground a massive white villa.

"Up there I think," Mando said and Shelter nodded his silent agreement. There was Hector Villa, there were the Willits brothers, and down here on the beach was the madman who would try to take them on single-handedly. How, he had no idea. It was all very fine to plan on joining the gang, becoming one of them—but the plan ended abruptly at that point. No one had given Shelter any pointers on just how you went about subduing an army.

The surf rolled in to the beach, hissing as it withdrew. The moon painted the long, crescent shaped beach silver. They were into the shadow of the promontory now, and Shelter looked up, measuring it, trying to guess its defenses.

It was a hundred feet high at the pinnacle, running back to the low jungle-clad hills, perhaps a quarter of a mile long in all. There would be guards up there, and plenty of them. Villa could not be confident that the *federales* would not march against him. In fact, he probably expected it.

What did he have up there then? A couple hundred men, well armed with new repeating rifles, probably with bunkers dug out for protection, two gatling guns and a ton of explosives.

They were challenged before they ever reached the promontory. There was a stack of sea-pocked boulders to Morgan's left and from their shadows a guard called out.

"Halt right there, whoever you are. There are weapons

36

trained on you."

"All right, take it easy," Shell called back.

"Who are you?"

"Why, damn you," Morgan answered, "I'm Jim Pike."

"Who?"

"Pike!" Shelter said angrily. "Didn't Gato tell you I was on my way up?"

"Gato said nothing," the guard said dubiously.

"Too much cerveza, I guess," Shelter chuckled. The guard had emerged from the shadows, a tall, somber looking man with a scattergun in his hands, he looked Shelter over carefully.

"Yeah, that's Gato for you. Who are you anyway," the guard asked, his manner easing.

"Villa hired me to come down here and teach you boys how to make war." Mando sputtered something and Shelter glanced around sharply.

"Well, there's some of them that could use it," the guard allowed. "You ought to see them with those gatlings."

"When I get through, we'll have a fighting force, I guarantee it," Shelter said.

"You'd better get on up. You supposed to be there for supper?"

"If I can get up there," Shelter said with a laugh and the guard waved his arm.

"Go ahead. My name's Renaldo. If you need somebody who can follow orders and keep those boys in line, you ask for me."

"I will," Shelter promised. He heeled his horse and walked it on toward the trail which led up to the house on

37

the hill.

"Why did you tell him all of that?" Mando asked.

"To make sure we got through," Shelter answered.

"When they find out you've lied, it will go hard on us. Maybe they will not let us join. Maybe Gato Hernandez will be waiting up there. He did not look like a man to suffer insults."

"That's too bad for Gato," Morgan replied. "We don't have a chance of joining up if we can't see the man, do we? Besides, what I told him is partly true. I'll teach these men something about fighting." But perhaps they wouldn't like what Shelter Morgan would teach them.

"I don't know, Jim Pike. I like you. You saved my life, maybe. I wouldn't be here without your help, but I wonder who you are, what it is you want here."

"Do you? Don't wonder, Mando, it's better that way."

"You are not a lawman?" the kid asked, coming too close to the truth.

"No, not that," Shelter said with a laugh which sounded false to his own ears. "Don't worry, Mando, we're together. Or, we are if you want to be. If you don't want to have anything to do with me, then let's part right now, we can go in separately."

Mando considered it, but decided that his chances of being accepted by Villa were better with this obviously experienced and bold American.

They could see the house now, white in the moonlight, beyond the dark, twisted cypress trees that grew along the flanks of the jutting promontory.

There were two more guards along the trail now, and an iron fence across it.

"Halt." They stepped out in unison, rifles lowered.

"Get out of the way. I'm Jim Pike, and I'm already late for supper."

There was a moment's hesitation, but the guards opened the gate and stood sullenly aside. Obviously anyone who had gotten through down below was all right. The name Jim Pike meant nothing to them, but the way the man spoke, it was apparently supposed to.

Shelter rode on through, a very nervous Mando behind him, glancing back at the guards. They emerged from the trees now and came up onto the flat back of the promontory. To their left were a dozen low buildings, some with lighted windows, the sounds of talking men drifting from them. There was smoke rising from several chimneys, the smell of meat cooking. Across a large expanse of open ground to the right was the house itself. Lofty behind adobe walls and pine trees it stood overlooking the moon glossed sea. It was of three stories, the windows iron barred, the roof red Spanish tile. From the house came the drifting notes of a piano being inexpertly played.

Shelter got down from his horse and dusted off, Mando studying him from horseback.

"What are you doing?"

"We're going in to meet the boss," Shell said.

"Tonight? Dressed like this? There is a party going on."

"All the better."

"Maybe we should look for someone else, not Villa himself," Mando suggested unhappily.

"Maybe so. Do what you want, Mando. I'm going to see Villa." And the Willits brothers? It was possible. Walk right through the front door like an idiot and find

39

himself face to face with Zack Willits. Maybe the killer wouldn't recognize his former captain. The eyepatch and whiskers might help. Then again, he might be alert for Shelter Morgan on his back trail. Willits might have heard what had happened to the others. To General Custis, to Colonel Fainer. There was only one way to find out for sure. Shelter looked at Mando and asked, "Ready?"

The kid wasn't ready, never would be. Nor would he ever be a soldier. Morgan could see him struggling with conflicting emotions. He wanted badly to see Villa, to enlist in his bandit army, yet he didn't have the nerve to walk in like this.

"What ever you say is right, Jim Pike," he replied, trusting to the older man.

There were other guards at the open head-high wooden gate leading into the grounds, but they operated on the same theory as those below had. The man had gotten this far, he must be all right. They stood back as Shelter led his horse through, Mando following uncertainly.

The piano playing had stopped, and they heard a man's laughter. The front of the house was ablaze with light. Half a dozen sleek, blooded horses were tied up before the house where a Mexican in a dark suit stood, hands behind his back, staring gloomily out at the sea.

Shelter walked straight up to the Mexican. "Watch our horses, will you? Might loosen the cinches and water them."

"Yes, señor," the man said without hesitation, and Mando gawked. Whoever Jim Pike was, he had his share of nerve. Mando swung down and stood nervously, straw hat in hand.

"Let's go," Shelter told him. He was already starting

40

for the door and Mando scrambled after him, not wanting to be left alone.

There was a huge bronze clapper on the door and the pull rope to a bell. Shelter ignored both. He opened the huge door and stepped into the lighted foyer of the big house of Hector Villa, bandit, revolutionary, killer.

4.

There was a dinner party going on. Three men in dress suits, ruffled shirts and polished boots lounged in the comfortable red plush chairs, looking toward the piano in the far corner. As Morgan, Mando at his heels, entered the house, his bootheels clacking on the tile floor, heads came around sharply. All of the men were Mexican. A slightly heavy man with pouched eyes and thinning hair sat to Morgan's left, glaring coldly at Shell. At his waist was a Remington revolver in a custom made holster. To Shell's right sat a lean, dangerous looking man with a clipped mustache, his hair streaked with silver, his eyes obsidian, cold. And before Shelter sat the master. Villa. He needed no introduction. He rose from his chair, alert as a big cat, his lips compressed, his eyes searching. He was of average height, wide across the shoulders, handsome in the Spanish mold—olive complexion, straight nose, flat cheekbones. There was something lurking in his eyes which suggested passion, danger, violence, and perhaps madness.

"Who are you?" Villa asked quietly. He did not shout, grow excited. He was doubly dangerous. A man who loses his temper reveals himself; Villa revealed nothing. He was in control, and Shelter had the feeling that Villa's reaction would have been essentially the same had a hundred federales burst into his house.

"Jim Pike," Morgan said, looking at the other two men. The heavy one he took for a politician, a local bigwig perhaps. The tall man was lean as a whip, a fighting man.

"The name means nothing. How did you get in here? What do you want?"

"Why, my friend and I want to work for you, Villa. We heard you needed fighting men."

"In the Estados Unidos you heard this?" Villa asked, coming nearer to size up the stranger, a glass of wine in his hand.

"That's what I heard, yes. I heard that you had yourself a war, that you had some soldiers, but they weren't worth a damn. That they didn't know one end of a rifle from the other taken all in all. That they were willing to fight—most of them—but they didn't know how."

"And so you have come to take command," Villa said with the barest trace of a smile. He was nearly face to face with Morgan now. Shell could smell the wine on his breath, the pomade on his hair.

"That's right."

"And this is your aide?" Villa asked looking at Mando who had gone white.

"Yes. His name's Mando Sandoval."

"What is this ridiculousness?" the tall man asked, rising from his chair now.

"My general, Arturo Realto," Villa said without shifting his eyes from Shelter's face.

"Who is this man?" Realto demanded. "Throw him out."

"I wish to talk to him, perhaps," Villa said.

"Is this the time, the place?" Realto asked.

43

"If I say it is," Villa responded coldly and Realto flinched. "You have been a soldier?" he asked Shelter.

"Most of my life."

"You can operate the gatling gun?"

"Of course, and any other weapon you care to name from flintlocks to artillery pieces."

"Ask him how he got in here," Realto demanded.

"I got in here because your men aren't careful enough," Morgan replied. "They need to have some lessons drummed into their heads."

"*You* can do this?" Realto scoffed.

"That's right. If I teach them, they'll learn. If I tell them, they'll do it."

"They do not like gringoes."

"They don't have to. I'm not going to throw them a tea party."

"You think you can control men such as ours?" Realto asked mockingly.

"Like who? Like Gato Hernandez? Yeah," Shelter drawled, "I can control them. I controlled Gato tonight when he decided Villa's army was nothing more than a riff-raff gang of thieves and he tried to rifle my belongings."

"This is true?"

"Ask him."

Realto snorted. Villa continued to look intently into Morgan's blue eyes. "Have you eaten?" Villa asked unexpectedly.

"I wouldn't mind a glass of wine," Shelter answered. Realto turned away with disgust.

"Sit then, let us talk for a while. Then," Villa said with a wisp of a smile, "I shall better be able to decide whether to hire you, Mister Jim Pike, or—kill you."

44

"Sounds fair," Shelter said evenly and Villa nodded with apparent approval. Realto had seated himself in a chair, hands dangling over the arms loosely. The fat man had risen and he now stood clutching his hat nervously. At the mention of murder he had begun to look ill as if Villa's dinner had not set well.

"I must leave," he said.

"So soon, Mayor?" He turned to Shelter. "The mayor of Escebar does not know what to do about me. He wishes to not antagonize me, yet I am a problem to him. He wishes me gone and yet he is paid well so long as I stay, is that not correct, Mayor?"

"I like to consider that we are friends," the mayor said unconvincingly. "The money is appreciated, but . . ."

"Go," Villa said. "I am not in the mood for your boot licking."

The mayor turned, his jaw twitching with suppressed anger, and walked past Shelter toward the door. Villa laughed harshly, and Morgan thought a little maniacally.

"Sit down, Mister Jim Pike."

"I think the kid would like to get some rest," Morgan said indicating Mando.

"Does not your aide attend your conferences?"

"He's just a kid I picked up along the way. He wanted to fight for you. I brought him."

"Very well. Go to the gate. Talk to Cruz. He will show you where to bed down."

Mando nodded and muttered a *"Si, señor,"* appearing both relieved and hurt to be excluded. The talk of killing had shaken him. He bowed out, walking swiftly toward the door as if afraid they would call him back.

"Now then, Mister Pike," Villa said, walking to the sideboard to remove a crystal goblet, examine it and fill it

45

with port wine from a cut-crystal decanter, "will you tell me exactly how you believe you can improve my soldiers' skills?"

Shelter began to do so, laying out a basic plan of training, familiarization with weapons, drill and combat skill, emphasizing discipline, always discipline—Villa had perked up the first time Shelter mentioned it and so he mentioned it again. Villa apparently liked discipline. If it was up to him the whole world would have been more disciplined, disciplined to obey Hector Villa.

Morgan had gotten down to his ideas about cavalry drill when the piano began to play again, that same loose melody, the same inexpert hunting for chords, and he turned around to see her sitting at the piano bench.

Tall, lovely, with dark hair, green eyes, wearing a white brocaded gown which plunged in front, revealing firm white breasts. She did not turn as Shelter stared at her, but he realized she knew he was staring at her. So did Villa.

"My mistress," he said, "Bonita Madrid."

Madrid. Shelter was stunned. He tried to put his mask back in place before Villa could guess the shock the name Madrid had produced.

Madrid, the agent in place. Villa's mistress. She continued to play softly and Shelter turned back to Villa. He had forgotten where he was and had to backtrack in the conversation. Villa was looking at him oddly now, seeing something.

"She is very beautiful, my Bonita Madrid," the bandit leader said.

"Yes."

"She belongs to me," Villa said with a little more steel in his voice.

46

"I can see that." That answer seemed to pacify Villa and after pouring another glass of wine he leaned back in his chair to listen to Morgan.

An hour later Villa rose and walked to where Realto sat sullenly in his chair. The revolutionary asked his general, "Well, what do you think? Keep him or kill him."

"Kill him," Realto said without a moment's hesitation.

"I think not," Villa said and Shell's hand relaxed, slipping back away from his holstered Colt. "Jim Pike is a soldier. What he says is true, not to diminish your achievements, Realto, but our discipline is not good. Our skills are only moderate. You will recall Jamale Wells . . ."

"Just because Ybarra's men broke and ran . . ."

"And others would have if we hadn't stood behind them with a gatling gun, urging them forward. They do not understand the ideals behind this glorious revolution. They do not understand that some men must die."

But never, Shell thought, the leaders. Never the Realtos and the Villas.

"The men will not follow an American. Look at those other gringoes."

"But Jim Pike is not a drunken oaf like the Willits brothers, are you, Jim Pike?"

"No." Shelter felt his skin flush, felt his adrenalin begin to flow. They were here after all, the Willits brothers were still with Villa.

"No, Jim Pike is not like them. Call Gato Hernandez, will you, Realto. I wish to speak to him. I wish to have him meet Jim Pike again."

"I do not agree with this decision," Realto said.

"You do not have to!" Villa flared up, showing temper for the first time. That apparently was the one thing he could not tolerate—subordinates telling him what to do. Realto was silently fuming, and maybe that was for the best. If Shelter was reading Villa right, it would only make the revolutionary leader more obstinate, more determined to use "Jim Pike" in his army.

The piano playing suddenly stopped and Bonita Madrid got up from the bench to walk toward them. Both men rose and she smiled warmly, beautifully, not at either man, but between them. She stood beside Villa, lightly holding his arm.

"I am tired. I must go up to bed now. Do not be long, my darling," she said to Villa who patted her hand and assured her he wouldn't.

She didn't look at Morgan, gave no sign that she knew who or what he was. She was very good at her trade, this one, and Shelter gave her deserved admiration. Admiration for her skills and for her beauty. His eyes fixed on her softly swaying hips, the dark, lustrous hair, the tantalizing walk as she moved away from them toward the wrought-iron railed staircase at the back of the room.

They sat down again after Bonita was gone. Villa's eyes were faraway, glassy as a different mood settled. Shelter, watching him, was certain of one thing—Villa could never be trusted to do anything. He was unpredictable, and probably insane. They sat in silence until Realto returned with Gato Hernandez.

Gato entered the house chatting, but when he saw Shelter he stiffened, falling silent, his hands bunching menacingly. Villa noticed it and seemed to delight in it. His mood changed swiftly again, his eyes brightened and he rose.

"Welcome, Hernandez. I believe," he said maliciously, "that you know Mister Jim Pike."

"Yes," Gato said uncertainly. His slow mind was trying to sort through this. Jim Pike had told him in Escebar that he was coming to take command of the training. Then, Gato had believed it to be bluff. Now he was here, in Villa's house, drinking Villa's wine. Who was he? He tried to put a lid on his simmering anger.

"I have met Mister Jim Pike."

"Where?"

"In Escebar this evening," Gato said, eyeing the wine decanter thirstily.

"Oh?" Villa acted unconcerned. "Did you speak?"

"Yes, we spoke," Gato answered.

Villa nodded, pouring yet another glass of wine. His back was to Gato when he asked, "What was it you talked about, Gato?"

"There was some trouble."

"Trouble?"

"Some of the men were curious to see what was in Mister Jim Pike's saddlebags. They had opened them when Pike came out of the restaurant." Gato was trying to side-step a little until he saw how things lay. Some of the men had been in Pike's saddlebags, but not Gato.

"Then what happened?" Villa asked. He had lighted a thin cigar. Now he tilted his head back and exhaled a stream of bluish tobacco smoke.

"Mister Pike asked that his things he put back," Gato mumbled.

Villa, who knew his men, could read behind Gato's words easily. They had tried to hold up the gringo and the gringo had braced them. Gato's men had backed down.

"How many men?" Villa asked casually.

49

"Six men, Señor Villa."

"And Pike had only his peon with him, the boy?"

"Yes, Señor Villa," Gato said with growing gloominess.

Villa nodded to himself then turned toward Realto who had maintained a cold silence. "Jim Pike will take charge of the training tomorrow, General."

"Yes, Señor Villa," Realto answered stiffly.

"Do you understand, Gato?"

"Yes."

"Very well, show Pike a cabin where he can stay. Inform your men that Pike will assume his duties immediately."

"Yes, Señor Villa."

"For now, good night, Pike. We shall see what you can accomplish."

Shelter followed Gato out into the yard. The moon was high, the shadows beneath the trees dark. Shell glanced back toward the house, at the light in one of the upstairs windows. Just for a moment he saw her silhouetted there—Bonita Madrid.

When Shelter looked away he noticed that Gato's eyes were on him. Neither man said a word until they had walked out the gate, leading their horses, and were approaching the cluster of buildings opposite.

"How long do you think you will last?" Gato asked.

"We'll see."

"The men will not stand for this."

"You mean you won't," Shelter replied.

"Maybe that is what I mean, Jim Pike, it is the same thing."

"Which one is my cabin?" Shell asked. To his left, back among the trees were three long low buildings,

50

barracks. To his right were half a dozen disconnected adobe cottages.

Gato muttered something under his breath and led the way toward the farthest one. Inside the cabin was musty, cobwebbed. There was a low frame and leather-strap bunk with a thin mattress, the ticking leaking out, and two folded blankets. Outside of a rickety table and two chairs that was the extent of the furnishings.

"We rise at seven," Gato said.

"It'll be six from here on," Morgan said. Gato stiffened and for a moment Shell thought the bandit was going to leap at him. He slowly relaxed and nodded.

"Bueno."

"Listen, Gato, I'm going to make it a little tough for the men because that's the only way I know to instill discipline, and discipline is sorely needed. It's something that has to be done for the good of the cause, for Villa. Understand?"

"I understand," Gato said, and there was a cold little light in his black eyes. "I understand very well."

With that Gato left, closing the door none too gently behind him. Morgan tossed his gear on the floor and looked around the cottage. He thought about starting a fire, but the chimney was likely clogged up if it had been maintained like the rest of the place. There was owl sign spattered about and Shell figured they probably had a nest up the chimney. Besides it was late and he was tired. It had been a lousy, long day. Tomorrow promised more of the same.

He placed his pocket watch on the table, kicked off his boots and crawled onto the sagging bed, hands behind his head. He lay there staring at the door for a long time, thinking of Gato and the Willits brothers, and of the

51

briefly viewed, feminine silhouette he had seen in Villa's upstairs window.

Then he fell to an uneasy sleep, dreaming dreams of blood and smoke. He was back in Georgia again, again seeing the death descend, the gunsmoke roll across the clearing, Welton Williams going down to be trampled by his horse, and looming out of the clouds of smoke, the ugly, round face of Zack Willits.

5.

Shelter was up early and out in the yard when the sun was just a reddish promise out at sea. He stood looking at the sea, at the small white town of Escebar for a minute then turned, following his nose toward the cookshack. The soldiers were stumbling bleary-eyed from the bunkhouses. To the man they appeared hungover. That would stop too. If Morgan was going to maintain his role of Jim Pike, war instructor, he was going to have to try to whip these bandits into shape. They were killers every one, but they weren't soldiers.

Shelter opened the door to the grub hall and walked in. Silence descended on the place. Rows of dark faces looked up from the plank tables to study "Jim Pike," the gringo with the whip hand.

Shelter saw Mando, looking very young and uncomfortable in a uniform three sizes too big for him. The kid averted his eyes, perhaps not wanting to be identified with Shelter. Shell walked across the room and took a seat at the table.

"You the tough man?"

Shelter looked up into the eyes of a red-eyed, bearded man. He was hovering over Shell, his sour stink in Morgan's nostrils. He was big and mean and ready.

"What's your name, soldier?" Shell asked and the

53

bandit laughed.

"You talk like you going to be in charge of us. You aren't. You won't be here very long, I promise you."

"I asked you what your name was," Shell said, and the soldier looked again at the tall man with the eye patch, suddenly wary.

"Tell him, Carlos!" someone laughed and the nasty, determined gleam returned to the bandit's eyes.

"I tell you nothing," Carlos said, leaning still nearer, his face inches from Shelter's. "I will do nothing you tell me. I don't take no orders from you."

"Then you can get your butt out of this camp," Shelter said evenly. "I'm taking charge and you're following orders. Or," he shrugged, "you can get gone. I don't really care which way it is."

"Maybe I don't go, maybe I don't take orders," Carlos said. "And what do you do about that, eh?"

Shelter showed him. He came up out of his seat, leading with a right hand hook which landed flush on the bandit's face. He staggered back, knocking plates from the table, crashing into three other bandits who shoved him back toward Morgan. Shelter caught him with a stiff left as he came in. Carlos goggled at Shell and then went down, hard. He hit the deck and lay there, looking at nothing, a thin trickle of blood running from his nostril.

Shelter sat down again. "Is there anything to eat around here?"

Outside the men formed up in a scruffy rank, their sergeants standing before them. Morgan looked them over scornfully. They didn't even know how to stand at attention.

"But you," Morgan told himself, "are going to whip

54

them into shape, make good fighting men out of these killers." No, he wasn't going to do that; it couldn't go that far. He was at Escebar to dismantle this machine, not to oil and adjust it to make it more efficient at what it did—killing.

Morgan got them into rough shape and spent the morning drilling them, noticing that Villa had arrived on a black horse to sit in the shade of the trees, watching.

At noon Morgan dismissed them, giving them the news. "There's not going to be any more drinking in the barracks." That produced a moan they could have heard down in the town. Morgan ignored that too and turned his back on them, striding away, nodding to Gato to dismiss them.

He caught up with Mando before the kid reached the barracks. "Mando! Wait up."

"What is it, Jim Pike?" Mando asked uneasily. He looked around at the other soldiers who passed them.

"I don't want you in that barracks. You can stay in the cabin with me."

"Must I?"

"What's the matter? A lot of talk about me?"

"They don't like you. They know I arrived with you and so they do not like me. Please, Jim Pike, I just want to be a good revolutionary soldier."

"You like these men, do you? Are they what you expected? Noble soldiers fighting for a cause?"

"They are all right. Please now, Jim Pike, I must go into the barracks."

"All right." Shelter looked at him. The kid wouldn't meet his eyes. "Go on then—but listen to me. You tell me when you don't want to be a soldier anymore, and I'll get you out of here. Do you understand?"

55

"No," Mando answered, "I do not understand. Now I must go, goodbye, Jim Pike."

"Your friend does not like your discipline either, eh?"

"What do you want, Gato."

"Villa wishes to see you at the big house."

"What's up?"

"Villa will tell you." Gato's expression gave nothing away. Shelter shrugged and started for the house.

The guards at the gate stood at attention as he passed through and Shelter smiled. He thought maybe Jim Pike should have himself a uniform made. What rank? Major, colonel? Maybe he and Villa could design some medals and award them to each other.

He knocked on the door of the big house and it swung open immediately. Bonita Madrid was standing suddenly in front of him, her faint lilac scent delicate and enticing, her dark eyes shining. He felt her hand touch his, felt her press a folded piece of paper into it.

"Ah, Morgan," Villa said appearing in the foyer. "Come in." His eyes went to Bonita and then back to Morgan, and Shelter didn't like the speculative expression there. It passed away quickly however. Villa put his arm around Shell's shoulder, leading him into his study. Bonita went out into the garden.

"I saw you this morning. I am pleased. The men have given you trouble?"

"Not much. Yet." Morgan smiled.

"They will not like having their mescal taken away," Villa answered, "but I am glad you have done this. What I wanted to talk to you about is more practical training."

"Such as?" Shell settled into an easy chair as Villa paced the room, hands behind his back.

56

"We have problems with some of our neighbors. They have attacked our supply trains, some men have been murdered."

"The people of Escebar?"

"No," Villa laughed. "Not those mice. The Tamaulipas. Do you know them?"

"The Indians."

"Yes, the jungle Indians. We have had dealings with them, but now they have become troublesome."

"You want to make war on them."

"Yes."

Shelter felt disgust rising in his belly, but he fought it down. Many thoughts ran through his mind—chief among them was the knowledge that Villa's men could train for a hundred years and never be able to fight a winning war against the Tamaulipas in that jungle where stealth and a knowledge of terrain was all.

"Why not?" Morgan said.

"I am especially interested that my men learn to operate the gatling guns we have. We will need them when we . . ." Villa's sentence trailed off. When he what? What did the man have in mind after he had his gunnery practice on some simple Indians?

"What about the other American soldiers you have?" Shelter asked casually. "Can't they operate those gatlings?"

"No. Only one was a soldier, by the way, and when he was in the army they had no such weapon."

No, they hadn't had any gatling guns. They'd had damn few repeating rifles. And nothing much in the way of footwear and blankets.

"Where are they, by the way?" Shelter asked.

"Away on business. They will be back soon. Possibly after you have completed your training mission." Villa's eyes narrowed. "Why are you so curious?"

"Just wondered. Thought it might be nice to have another American around to talk to."

"You would not enjoy talking to the Willits brothers. They are ignorant louts. Vicious, dirty men. Sometimes I think . . ."

Again he left his thought unfinished. Shelter watched the man as he poured a glass of wine, not his first of the day judging by the glossiness of the eyes, the flush on his cheeks. He looked a little unsteady, did this emperor. Twice he had said just a little more than he had intended. How much was he drinking? Shell wondered.

Shelter tried gently to milk the man. "What is our ultimate objective, sir?"

"Why do you ask such a question?"

"If I know what sort of task the men will have to perform, it will facilitate training. For example, if I were to teach them the techniques of desert fighting and then find that we were intending to storm a mountain stronghold, the training would have been wasted, worse, it would be detrimental."

"I see. I hadn't thought of it in that way," Villa said, downing his drink so hastily that it spilled on his chin and trickled down his throat. Villa, if he noticed it at all, paid no heed to it.

"My ultimate objective is quite simple," he said, "I want all of Mexico."

"All of Mexico." Morgan repeated but Villa seemed not to hear him.

"My army is small now. We have not even taken

58

control of this province. The Indians resist us and there are counter-revolutionaries in Escebar. I know this. But we shall have control in time, and as we move our army will grow. All of the peasants in this nation will flock to our cause." Villa's eyes positively glittered now. His face had grown crimson with passion. He quickly poured and drank more wine. "This will happen—I can see it clearly. A vision of the future, my friend, and those who are loyal to me now will be richly rewarded.

"You, Pike," he said, his mood changing abruptly. "Are you loyal to me?"

"Of course, Señor Villa."

"Yes, I think so. Realto says we should have no Americans here, no foreigners. He says they fight only for gain, not out of loyalty. Yet what is Realto himself here for?" The question didn't call for an answer and Morgan made no reply. "No, Jim Pike, money can buy the greatest kind of loyalty, and the promise of more wealth can retain this loyalty." He came nearer to Shelter, looking directly at him, yet it was as if Villa somehow did not see him. "I will make you wealthy beyond dreams. All of us. You must believe it."

"I do," Morgan said and the sound of his voice yanked Villa out of his trance. He wiped a hand across his eyes and said:

"See to the Indian war."

"Yes, Señor Villa."

Morgan whistled under his breath as he reached the front porch. He had seen the instability in Villa before, but he hadn't realized how deep it went. He was plain mad, something upstairs had come loose and tilted over. Now it was sliding loose, and rapidly.

Morgan walked back to his cottage, closed the door and then took the note Bonita Madrid had given him from his pocket.

"I must see you tonight. The old greenhouse.
Madrid"

Shelter read the note again then walked to the fireplace, and lighting a match he touched the flame to the paper, turning it so that it burned the note to ashes. When it was completely consumed he stepped on the ashes, grinding them under his boot sole.

Then he returned to his bunk and lay down on his back, watching the ceiling. Who was Bonita Madrid anyway? How could she stand to live with a madman like Villa, duty or not? She was his mistress; how could she sleep with the likes of him? Or was she that callous that it didn't matter. Just a part of the job?

Still thinking of Bonita Madrid, remembering the line of her jaw, the sleek neck, the swell of her breasts, Shelter fell to sleep.

He awoke refreshed an hour later. Going to the window he stood looking through the trees at the collection of ramshackle outbuildings behind the big house. If one of them had ever been a greenhouse, he couldn't tell it.

Snatching up his hat Shell went out, looking for Gato. He found him behind one of the bunkhouses, watching the men break a string of horses.

"Can I talk to you?" Shell asked.

Gato turned toward him, surly and suspicious. He was obviously still nursing a grudge, as was the man behind him leaning against the corral pole—Carlos, his nose swollen, his eye encircled by a purple bruise.

"What is it?"

"Villa wants the men to have some practice with the gatlings. Bring them out in the morning, will you? Clips and ammunition."

"All right."

"I thought maybe we could use one of those old buildings for a target. What in hell are they anyway?"

"The largest was a pavillion where the don who owned this house once held his dance parties. He had three lovely daughters, a lovely old world wife. The white building with half a roof was a greenhouse. He had glass brought from Spain—it took a full year."

"Must have been nice." Shelter, looking at the old buildings now could almost envision the greenhouse whole, the pavillion lighted by Chinese lanterns one spring evening, the Spanish girls dancing with their young men.

"What happened to the buildings?"

"Cannon." Gato shrugged. "When we offered to buy the house, the old don refused."

"So Villa took it."

"What else. There were orders not to hit the big house, though."

"And the old don? What happened to him?"

"What would you imagine?" Gato asked with a leering grin. "Dead. And the wife—an accident that, she stepped in front of the old man while we were shooting him, and so she was gone too, the Señora Madrid."

"Madrid?"

"Yes, did you not know? The old man was Don Alberto Madrid. The girl in the house," Gato lifted his chin, "is his daughter."

Shelter returned to the cottage, thinking black

61

thoughts. He knew something now of Bonita Madrid, and he could imagine the terrible anger which must be alive and writhing beneath that cool, beautiful exterior. No wonder she stayed—this was her home. No wonder she was working against Villa. She must live for the day she would see him hung.

Bonita hadn't mentioned a time in the note. Probably it would have to be late, when Villa was in his cups, snoring a drunkard's snore. He watched the sky go dark, his eyes on the ruined old greenhouse, his thoughts on the woman he was going to meet.

His patience exhausted, Shelter slipped out of the cottage an hour later and began moving through the shadows toward the greenhouse. There was only one light burning in the big house that Shell could see from this side. A light there, one in the bunkhouse behind him and the pale light of the rising moon. The rest of the world was dark and silent.

He could see the broken form of the greenhouse against the lighter sky and he worked toward it over broken masonry and brush. He settled down on a garden bench which had been left intact beside a huge old cypress tree, and he waited.

The moon slowly rose, the shadows beneath the tree growing dimmer. There was no one there, and then there was.

He saw her softly floating across the yard toward him, the sea breeze twisting the sheer white garment she wore around her, toying with her long dark hair.

Shelter, trained by bitter experience not to be too trustful, watched the shadows behind her, waiting to see another shadow, a more deadly one. There was nothing there, no one behind her. The night was still and calm, the moon above the villa beaming down.

"I only have a minute." She reached him breathlessly, her breasts rising and falling beneath the filmy material of her gown.

"No one followed you?"

"Villa is dead to the world," she said breathing hard still. "As he always is at this time of the evening."

"All right, what's up?"

"You know about the maneuvers against the Tamaulipas?" She formed a bitter expression, her fine broad mouth twisting into an angry sneer. "What a pig. To hunt those people."

"Why is he?" Shell asked, his eyes running admiringly along the line of her shoulder, her smooth breasts.

"I don't know. Because they will not obey, because they attack his men, because he has to kill! I found this out this morning—he wants his men to learn to use the gatling guns because he plans on using them when he storms the army post at Tampico."

"When he what?" That seemed incredible even for Villa.

"Yes, I know, it is madness, but he has the men and the equipment to pull it off. That is his next plan, to destroy an army post, the whole town if he has to. He needs to prove his strength, a strength he does not possess in other areas," she said, looking at the ground.

"What do you mean?" Shelter asked.

"Haven't you guessed? He is impotent as a man."

"But you . . ."

"He keeps me out of pride. He shows me to other men and they believe things are different. Sometimes I think I will go mad living with the butcher, but as long as there is a chance I am helping to stop him, I will do so. Anything, to avenge my family!" she said and her voice was coldly passionate. She got control of herself and went on. "The Willits brothers are there—in Tampico, reconnoitering. They will be back tomorrow or possibly the next day. Then they will plan the battle. Or rather Realto will plan it. He is the only one who knows anything about military matters. I think sometimes that if Realto were not here, the army would fall apart."

"That's something to think about," Shell said to himself.

"I can't stay any longer," she said. She hesitated, started to say something and then unexpectedly got to tiptoes and kissed Shell on the lips. "Be careful. Stop this madman." Then she was gone, vanishing through the shadows of the cypress trees like a lovely ghost. Morgan stood there watching after her, wondering.

6.

Shelter was up before dawn the next morning and while the soldiers ate their breakfast he checked out the gatling guns which rested on twin caissons before the barracks. He stepped up and checked the action on the first gun, cranking the barrel over, noticing that it caught, probably needing a little grease. There were no sights attached, but then Shelter had always figured that sights on a gatling were like a silk hat on a mule.

There were two boxes of ammunition on each caisson, strapped to the bed just above the wheels. Shell opened each and checked the magazines.

"Everything all right?" the sarcastic voice asked and Shell looked up to find General Realto standing before him, resplendent in a uniform he had designed himself, one with lots of gold braid and shiny buttons.

"This one will do. I haven't looked at the other one yet."

"We'll be leaving in an hour," Realto told him.

"I thought we were going to have some lessons on these guns," Shell replied.

"We'll leave that for the field. I want to get moving. Villa wants the Tamaulipas punished. Last night four of our men were murdered in the jungle."

"All right. Have you thought about dynamite?" Shell

65

had—quite a bit. It was a very useful commodity and one side could use it as well as the other.

"Why?" Realto asked suspiciously.

"It might be useful in the jungle."

"We're saving it for . . ." For the army post at Tampico, he was about to say, but he didn't.

"Can't spare any?" Shell squatted back on his heels, tilting his hat back. The morning sun was warm on his back.

"I don't see why we need it."

"Training purposes, Realto. These men know anything about fuses or setting a charge? You can place a bundle of sticks against a wall and not do anything but make a bunch of smoke if you don't know what you're doing. It's not too damned difficult to blow yourself up either if you don't know how to handle the stuff."

Realto wavered and then agreed. "All right, I'll have Gato bring some along."

"Good. We'll show those Indians something, won't we," Shelter said and there was an undertone to his voice that Realto did not understand and didn't like. He looked sharply at Morgan and then turned away, swaggering in his new uniform. Shelter sat on his heels, watching the man, breaking into a grin.

He found Gato before Realto did. "We need some dynamite. The general wants to do some explosives training in the jungle."

"Maybe I better go ask him," Gato said.

"Maybe you just better take my word for it, Gato. Are we going to have to have another lesson?"

Gato started to flare up, then just muttered under his breath. He led Shell to a small shack beyond the cookhouse. Taking a key from his pocket he unlocked the

66

door and went on in. He returned with a box of dynamite, a box of fuses.

"Now are you satisfied?" Gato demanded.

"Yes." Now he was satisfied. Now he knew where the dynamite was.

The soldiers were forming up under Realto's supervision when Morgan returned, carrying his dynamite. The general shot him a searching glance, but said nothing as Morgan strapped the crate onto the caisson. Shelter saw Mando in the ranks, looking smaller and younger. He hadn't found much romance in this yet, apparently. He would have to find a way to get Mando separated from the rest of the soldiers when the shooting started. If he'd had any sense, Shelter decided, he would have left the kid stranded on the desert without a horse, leaving him no choice but to try walking home.

"One hour," Realto called up to Shelter. "You'd better get your horse and get ready."

Morgan nodded and jumped down from the caisson. As he did he saw the four riders coming into the camp from the beach trail. Shell felt his mouth tighten, felt his gut lift and contract.

Four men, all similar in appearance, and the man in the lead he knew, knew too well. The Willits brothers were back. They glanced without curiosity at the ranks of soldiers, and Shell saw Zack Willits' eyes flicker as his gaze sept over Shell. Was it curiosity or knowledge? Some memory nudged in the dull mind of the killer? Something about the one-eyed, bearded man which seemed too familiar.

"One hour, Pike," Realto said, "get moving now."

"All right." Shelter turned toward his cottage, not glancing back at the four Americans. For the time being he was safe. Zack hadn't recognized him. If he had, the big man would have ridden him down, pumping his body full of bullets. He would have to, because he would know. Know that Shelter Morgan had exactly the same kind of fate in mind for Willits.

Shell saddled the gray and led it back to the yard where the caissons were having horses harnessed to them. Shell sat looking at the big house, wishing he could just trudge up there and settle the old score with Willits.

There were other things to be considered now, however. Like a tribe of Indians who were going to be massacred if Villa had his way, like the dark-eyed woman who lived a prisoner in that house.

"Ready?" Realto asked, and Shelter nodded. "One of the other Americans is coming," the general added. "Soon he will come."

Shelter felt his mouth go dry. Zack Willits was going along. But it wasn't Zack. It was a younger, even larger version of Zack who arrived a few minutes later. A big, ugly, vicious man with a perpetual scowl on his face, he was introduced to Morgan.

"Hardy Willits, this is Jim Pike, a countryman of yours."

"What's your game, Pike?" Hardy asked sourly.

"Same as yours. Just trying to pick up a little loose change," Shelter told him with a smile. Hardy Willits did not smile in return. Hardy Willits, Shelter decided, was not a smiling man.

He sat his horse next to Morgan, still staring at him. He was big and confident. His shoulders filled his blue shirt to bursting. He was massive through the chest. He had killed men and he would kill again if he got the chance. Shelter didn't mean to give him the chance.

68

Realto shouted out a command and his soldiers began marching down the beach road, the caissons and supply wagon rolling along behind them. Shelter and Willits tailed after them.

"Now we make a little war, huh?" Willits said, but he seemed to be talking to himself, and Shelter didn't answer. Yes, he thought, now we make a little war.

Only Morgan's war wasn't going to be exactly the same as Willits'. Willits, Realto and Villa had in mind a little gunnery practice, a little harmless slaughter. What Shell planned to do was more in the nature of guerilla warfare. He meant to take on this army single-handedly, and if he couldn't kill it, he felt sure he could cripple it well enough to save at least a few lives. He looked again at Willits. "And maybe take a few in the bargain," he thought.

They passed through Escebar at noon, the townspeople peering out of their windows, around corners, not knowing what was up, only knowing that they didn't want it to happen there. In another two hours they were into the jungle and suddenly Realto seemed to have no idea what he wanted to do. Where were the Tamaulipas? He almost seemed to have expected the Indians to come forward and line themselves up in front of the gatling guns.

The trail narrowed and it became impossible for the supply wagon to continue. They had to cut back jungle growth to allow the narrower caissons to pass. They were sticky with heat; the mosquitoes had begun to swarm and all of their weapons were useless against them.

Morgan found Realto as the caissons had again bogged down. The general was cursing, waving his hands in the air in red-faced anger.

"Realto?"

"What is it?" he demanded spinning to face Shelter.

"I've got a suggestion."

"What?" He turned again on his men, "Not like that—get a plank under that wheel."

"I wanted to go out and have a look around, Realto. Do a little scouting. Without some sort of reconnaissance we haven't got much hope of even finding the Indians, let alone defeating them."

"Perhaps." Realto removed his cap and wiped his brow. His new uniform, Shelter noticed, was already sweat-soaked and stained. "What did you have in mind?"

"Just myself and another man. I thought I'd take Willits along unless you want to come yourself."

"No," Realto said hastily. "I can't go, obviously. Take Willits. We'll camp up ahead in that clearing—there's not much hope of traveling farther before dark anyway."

"All right. Post sentries, Realto."

"I obviously planned to," Realto said, getting up a head of steam again.

Shelter turned on his heel and left the general to berate the men trying to free the caisson. He found Willits and told him, "Realto wants you and me to go out and scout around a little bit."

"The hell he does!" Willits snarled. "Why us? I was planning on eating and getting some sleep."

"I couldn't tell you why," Morgan said with a shrug. "All I know is those are his orders."

Willits sat glaring at Realto's back for a long minute. "Okay," he said finally. "I knew this was a mistake coming along."

"Why did you?" Shell asked, but Willits didn't

answer. He produced the closest thing to a smile he was capable of and shook his head.

"Let's go find some Indians, Pike."

Hardy Willits was almost eager as they left the camp, but as they moved into the jungle and darkness settled he began to balk.

"How in hell are we going to find anything in this tangle?" he growled.

"Keep your voice down," Shell said. They had gotten from their horses to proceed through some low hanging trees. A vine brushed against Shell's shoulder. At least he hoped it was a vine, remembering the snakes which infested the area.

"Let's get on back," Hardy said.

"Realto's orders."

"Yeah, Realto can screw himself."

"Quiet." Shelter had halted and Hardy Willits nearly bumped into him.

"What is it."

"Straight ahead. Maybe half a mile."

Willits squinted into the darkness and finally he picked it out, a faint reddish glow against the black background. "A campfire," he said.

"Has to be. Shall we take a closer look? "

"Don't seem smart to me," Hardy complained.

"It won't seem smart if we prepare an assault and find out after we get there that they aren't Tamaulipas at all," Morgan answered.

"Who else could it be?"

"Maybe we've been traveling in a circle and it's our own people."

"You're crazy," Willits growled. The big man was growing nervous and truthfully Shell couldn't blame him. They could be surrounded by Indians and they wouldn't have known it. Indians with silent poison darts.

"Come on."

Willits, grumbling and cursing under his breath followed along. They splashed across a narrow bog and entered a stand of mahogany trees. A night bird squawked a sudden complaint and Willits nearly came out of his skin.

"We'll have to leave the horses here," Morgan said.

He could see Willits' expression by the light of the coming moon, and it was not a pretty thing. The big man had his hand on his holstered pistol.

"What in hell are you up to?"

"I'm just trying to do the damned job we've been given, Willits. The horses are too clumsy, too noisy. I'm going ahead on foot, if you don't have the nerve, turn back toward Realto's camp."

"What are you talking about, nerve? I've got more nerve than you'll ever see, Pike."

"All right. I'm not here to argue with you. Are you coming along or not?"

"Yeah, I'm coming."

They left the horses tied loosely to the undergrowth and moved off afoot into the dense jungle. The moonlight appeared only infrequently, flooding the ground as it shone through the occasional gaps in the trees.

"I think we're heading the wrong way," Willits said. He was panting now as they climbed a low hill.

"No. Keep your voice down."

"What in the hell are you up to, Pike? I don't like this."

"Tough."

"God damn you." Willits grabbed Shelter's shoulder

72

and spun him around. "What did you bring me out here for? I don't trust you, Pike, not a bit."

Willits lifted his hand and Shelter didn't wait to find out what he had in mind. He kicked out hard, his boot-heel landing solidly on Hardy Willits' kneecap. The big man roared with pain and lunged at Shell.

Morgan felt the big hands of Willits close around his throat and he brought his own hands up between Willits' arms, knocking them away. Shell started to draw his Colt, but Willits, staggering into him, gripped Shelter's arm, brought his knee up, and the gun went flying.

Shelter dug a right into Willits' gut, but the blow seemed to have no effect on Hardy Willits. He clubbed at Shell with a fist as big as a ham, stunning him as the blow glanced off Morgan's temple.

Shelter fell back a step, saw Willits go for his own gun, and flung himself toward the shadows of the trees as Willits fired twice, the roar of the pistol amazingly loud in the jungle stillness. Morgan was up and running now, weaving through the trees. A third shot was fired. Morgan stopped and slipped through the undergrowth, hearing the heavy footsteps of Willits behind him.

Another bullet sang off the tree near Shell's head and he took off at a dead run, circling toward his horse across the low bog. Willits was pounding down the hill, massive and threatening. The moon illuminated his expression—malignant, enraged, purposeful.

Shelter came down the slope and started into the bog. He didn't get far. There was a deep hole where he was trying to cross and the suction was pulling him down into the stinking swamp. He looked around desperately and found the long root of the swamp magnolia. Using it he drew himself out of the waist-deep bog.

If it hadn't been for the root . . . Willits was coming through the undergrowth now, like a charging bull. Morgan looked upslope then bent to his work. He tore at the long slender root and finally got it doubled back on itself until it broke.

Taking a running start down the slope, Morgan hurled himself into the air. He managed to leap the bog, landing with one foot on solid ground. Willits had burst from the trees on the other side and a bullet plowed into the soft bank near Shell's face, spattering him with mud.

He clawed his way up the bank and into the trees, turning just in time to see Willits hesitate, take determination, and come charging down the slope. The big man leaped, but it wasn't far enough. He hit the bog dead center and slowly began to sink. He was already to his waist when Shelter emerged from the trees to stand watching.

"Pike! Help me!"

He was sinking slowly, inexorably. He was to his chest now, and all of his thrashing was only serving to sink him more quickly. He looked around desperately for something to grab hold of, but there was nothing.

His eyes were wide and white in his ugly face. His mouth was twisted with curses as the bog crept up to his chin. "Pike!" he screamed again before the mud and slime of the bog filled his mouth and Hardy Willits fell silent. In another minute there was no sign at all of Hardy Willits, no sign that he had ever existed.

"One down," Shelter muttered, wiping the slime and mud from his arms. One down and three to go. Shelter turned back toward his horse, walking slowly through the night-cloaked jungle.

When he rode back into Realto's camp an hour later he

74

unsaddled and rolled out his bed without reporting in. Realto, harried, weary, found him tugging off his boots.

"What happened?" the general demanded. "Where's Willits."

"The Indians got him," Shelter said shaking his head sadly. He said it loudly enough for anyone nearby who happened not to be sleeping to hear.

"You found their camp?"

"No. I'll try again tomorrow."

"Willits dead. His brothers . . . ! They will be grieved."

"Yeah, it's a great loss to the world," Shelter said, rolling up in his blankets. "He was a fine man."

Realto stood over the American a while longer, then worriedly shaking his head, he walked back toward his own bed. Shelter fell off to a deep and untroubled sleep.

7.

It was raining when Shell woke up the next morning. A light mist seeping through the trees to rise again as steam from the saturated earth. Through the dark ranks of trees Shell could see a narrow crimson band as the sun bled onto the clouds.

By the time they had eaten and started to move again, the rain had increased, driving down heavily, and they could see it meant trouble. Already the road was covered with water in places.

They had seen nothing of the Indians, although they knew they were out there, watching silently. Shelter rode his gray up beside Mando who was trudging forward through the mud, his young face showing strain.

"Hell of a romantic war, isn't it?"

"Leave me alone, Jim Pike."

"But then we haven't gotten to the fun part yet. Wait until we start blasting those Indians, huh?"

"Shut up, Jim."

"Why? Savor it all, I say. Wait until those gatling guns start shredding bodies. The only thing I don't get is how the Tamaulipas came to be enemies of the people? They seem to be pretty much out of the way, keeping to themselves. I thought maybe you could explain that to me, Mando."

"Go to hell!" Mando said savagely.

Shell's voice changed as he leaned over the withers of the gray. It softened and became compelling. "You know, Mando, this land looks somewhat familiar. We're near to the river, aren't we? It should be just over there. If a man was to start walking that way maybe he'd just keep on walking until he was back on the desert. Maybe he'd be home in a week or so, back with family and friends."

"Go away," Mando hissed and Shell, straightening up, held up the gray, letting the long line of Villa's soldiers pass. He found Realto at the rear of the column.

"Ground's real low ahead," he told the general. "Want me to see if I can't find another trail?"

"You are not afraid to go into the jungle alone?" Realto asked with a suspicious gleam in his eyes. "After what happened to the other American?"

"Indians don't bother me," Shelter answered. "I figure I can handle them."

"Go on then!" Realto snarled. "Get us out of this swamp. Let us find the Tamaulipas' camp and be done with this madness."

"Madness? Is that the word you used, Realto? Villa doesn't think it's madness." Chuckling, Morgan turned his horse and headed off through the trees, Realto glaring after him, knowing that his lips had betrayed him. One did not call Villa mad. It may be so, but one did not say it.

To Gato Hernandez Realto said, "I don't trust that man. I don't trust him and I do not like him."

"Perhaps he too will not come back from this battle," Gato suggested coldly. Gato didn't like Jim Pike either. He hadn't forgotten the humiliation.

Realto looked sharply at Gato and then slowly he smiled. "Perhaps not," the general said.

Shelter moved through the jungle, liking the rain, the shifting screen of clouds, the dark glossy leaves of the trees. The jungle thinned somewhat as he rode southwest toward the bulky peaks which thrust their heads through the clouds. Their flanks were filmed silver as water rushed off of the slopes. Somewhere an undaunted parrot shrieked out a defiant note.

Morgan came suddenly upon the trail. Narrow, winding, it appeared to lead up toward the high country. He frowned. There is always a reason for a road, and what reason could this one have for existing but to lead to the Indian village, or perhaps to their fields where maize and grains were cultivated?

He started up it all the same, and a few hundred yards on he found the first of the stones. It sat in a clump of knee-high metallic green fern. It was itself four feet tall, of ancient gray granite, four-sided. On it were inscribed odd characters in a language unlike any Morgan had encountered. He could make out the symbol for the sun, a disc with stylized rays fanning out from it. It was old, very old.

There was a second and then a third along the trail as he rode. Milestones? Religious shrines? He had no way of knowing. The trail had begun to wind up along the sides of the foothills. There was still much jungle, but some of the trees had been cleared off, or burnt off and the second growth hadn't yet taken over.

Morgan could see the broad silver band of the river where the sun, between lowering clouds, gleamed on it and far distant the indigo of the sea.

The trail suddenly forked and Shell sat his horse, trying to decide which was the right way. He took the left-hand fork and rounded a grassy hill where a rill ran burbling down through the rocks. The trail was good for a hundred yards and then it began to tilt ominously, the left-hand shoulder sagging downslope. Morgan halted the gray and climbed down, walking ahead.

Below there was a drop of a thousand feet to the jungle depths; above the grassy hill. When he walked a little farther on he saw that the trail was impossibly slanted. Good enough for a man afoot—if he had good balance—but hardly suitable for anything else.

Nodding with satisfaction Shelter walked back to the gray, swung aboard and headed back. He reached the fork in the road and rode a little ways up the right-hand trail, finding it dry, and relatively smooth. It wound for as far as he could see into the hills, rising toward the mist-shrouded peak beyond.

He turned and rode back toward the low ground and Realto.

The general was in a foul mood when Shelter found him at the rear of the column. The going was very bad, the ground boggy beneath a foot of standing water.

"Well?" Realto snapped.

"I found the village."

Realto brightened, then scowled suspiciously. "You are sure of this?"

"I'm sure. There's a good trail leading toward it. High and dry."

The second caisson had bogged in again and the entire column stopped. A dozen soldiers to their knees in water got behind the caisson and pushed the gatling free.

"Where is the trail?" Realto asked.

"The foot of it's a mile or so south. Once we cross the bog here, it's all good traveling. As the trail rises there's no problem with water."

Realto mopped his forehead with a handkerchief. The heat and humidity were oppressive. Perspiration streamed out of every pore. Realto sighed.

"All right. Gato is ahead. Tell him to follow you. Morgan—I hope you are not wrong about this. I hope Villa is not wrong about you," he said, the tone of his voice a warning.

"I'm in it for the money. As long as I know Villa will pay me, I'm a Villa man, don't you worry about it."

"A failure out here will look very bad for you," Realto warned him.

"Maybe not so bad as it would look for you, eh, Realto? After all I'm just an instructor, you're the general." Then he smiled thinly, an expression Realto didn't seem to care for much.

"Tell Gato which way to go," the general said angrily.

In an hour they were across the low ground and rolling along easily up the trail Shelter had scouted. Realto, he saw, was continuing to ride at the rear of the column, letting Gato take the lead. He had fallen into that habit while they were in the jungle below so that the men would have time to clear the trail with their machetes before Realto passed through. It suited Shelter's purposes perfectly.

At the head of the column Morgan saw Gato Hernandez, sitting his black horse, and he smiled. Maybe, just maybe.

He slowed his gray again, letting the column pass by.

"Anything the matter?" Realto asked as he saw Shelter waiting beside the trail.

"Not that I know of. The trail gets a little tricky ahead. We have to keep to the right-hand fork. I'll tell Gato before we reach it."

"You'd better tell him now," Realto said in a way which indicated he didn't care to talk to the one-eyed American any more.

"Maybe I'd better," Shelter said. "That left-hand road is a mess, if we try it we've got troubles."

He heeled the gray and moved at a lope toward the front of the column. Mando turned his head away as Shelter passed him.

"Gato!"

Hernandez turned with a deep scowl on his face, the blood vessels in his throat bulging. The man was ready, Shelter thought, ready to have another try at Morgan. The hatred in his eyes was unmistakable.

"What is it, Pike?" he demanded.

"Realto said I should tell you. There's a fork in the road ahead. Make sure you take the left-hand trail. The right's a treacherous piece of road."

"All right. You have told me. Is there anything else?" the Mexican said.

"Nothing else," Morgan replied. He tugged down his hat and grinned, watching as the column plodded on, the men exhausted and short-tempered, their uniforms muddy. This was not what they had hired on to do. Tramping through jungles in the rain, the object of their mission invisible and nebulous. Shelter watched their sullen faces, feeling not a bit of pity.

Except for one man. For the kid. Mando who obviously disliked this but felt ashamed to leave. To go home and say: "I'm not a soldier; Hector Villa is no friend of the people."

The wagons rolled on and Morgan sat his horse beside the trail. He could see a scowling Realto approaching and slowly the unhappy expression began to change

81

to anxiety.

"What in the hell is he doing!"

Shelter looked southward, knowing what he would see. The column had started down the left-hand fork.

"Didn't you tell him?" Realto demanded.

"Of course I did."

"Why is he taking that trail?"

Shelter shrugged. "You'd have to ask him—he acted like he didn't trust me to tell him which way was right and which was left."

"Stop him!"

"Yes, general," Morgan said, barely holding back his grin. He turned his horse, heeled it roughly and set off, mane and tail flying, knowing that it was already too late. As he rounded the bend in the trail out of Realto's sight he slowed his horse, yawned and walked it forward, surrounded by marching—if you could call that dragging weary gait marching—soldiers.

"Gato!" Shelter called out for show. "Stop, I told you the right-hand trail."

Ahead a shout went up and Shelter rounded the turn in the trail just as the first caisson, canted steeply toward the drop-off to the east began to go. The inside wheels lifted and the horses pulling it reared up in fright. Then it went.

It simply rolled off the trail, dragging the horses with it. The caisson yanked at the harness and the straps gave. The horses, sliding farther still, were free of the death trap. But the caisson kept rolling, the gatling gun riding it down to the deep jungle below as Gato stood cursing, waving furious arms.

"Pike! Damn you."

He rushed toward Shell, drawing his sidearm as he

came. Realto was coming up fast from the rear. Shell just sat his horse. If he drew his gun he was liable to be cut down by the Mexican soldiers, none of whom had a liking for him. So he just sat and waited as the red-faced, blustering Gato Hernandez approached.

"I ought to kill you! This is your fault."

"No. You ought to listen. I told you to take the right-hand trail."

"You are a liar." Gato was trembling with rage. Realto halted his horse next to Morgan. "He lied, General."

"Sure I lied," Morgan said in a low, cold voice. "I wanted to wreck that caisson so when we fought the Indians we'd all get ourselves killed—me with you. I want to wreck this army I'm trying to whip into shape so I can lose a good-paying job. I'm not lying, Gato—either you're stupid or you were just too bull-headed to listen to me. Besides that—look at the trail—anyone dumb enough to just keep on rolling after seeing what this trail looks like is an idiot. You shouldn't be commanding troops, you shouldn't even be in this army if this is how your thinking works!"

Shelter's voice had picked up some heat as he scored Gato Hernandez. Realto had just waited, listening, watching his two subordinates.

"Why did you continue on, Gato?" Realto asked quietly, looking at the slanted, broken trail. "Anyone can see this is the wrong way."

"It was your order! Or so I thought."

"Order? I ordered you to kill men, horses, to wreck equipment? I think Pike is right—your reasoning is less than adequate if you continued blindly along this trail. You should have held up and asked!"

"Yes, General," Gato said. But his eyes were on Shelter

83

Morgan—killing eyes. Gato had never liked him and now there was a mad hatred building in him.

Two of the soldiers had scrambled down the steep cut and were leading the horses up. One of them was limping badly.

"See if we can recover the caisson," Realto said to Gato.

"Yes, General."

"I don't know how you're going to back the other caisson off of here, but I suggest you give it serious thought. Now, Gato! Get your people moving."

"Yes, General," Gato replied as tonelessly as before. The pistol still dangled in his right hand.

Realto turned and rode away and Morgan and Gato were left to stare at each other. "I won't forget this, Pike. I promise you that."

"I'd be disappointed if you did, Gato," Morgan said with a smile which so infuriated Gato that for a moment Morgan thought he was going to bring that gun up and start shooting.

Instead he turned away and shouted to his men. "Cut the team loose from the caisson! Hitch on behind with saddle mounts! To the rear. Everyone to the rear."

Then Gato with two of his men, Shelter trailing along behind, climbed down the slope toward where the other gatling gun-carrying caisson had rolled.

They found it, shattered, both wheels broken, half submerged in a swampy depression. To take it out meant towing it through the jungle and up the slope. The horses couldn't be brought down it and there was just no way man power was going to do it. If they did get it up it would mean somehow carrying it on horseback and that just didn't seem likely.

"It's lost," Gato said surveying the situation morosely. "It's lost—Villa will have a fit."

Yes he would, a mad raving fit. A lunatic explosion, and Gato Hernandez was the one who was going to bear the brunt of it. Tough.

"Too bad," Morgan said.

Gato spun toward him, his eyes smoldering. He stood staring for a full minute, his jaw muscles working. Finally he turned and began to climb up through the jungle, his men following.

Shelter went to where the caisson lay tilted into the slime, and he unstrapped the ammunition box, the crate of dynamite. Dragging them back into the jungle for a hundred feet along a dim trail he hid them among a jumble of volcanic rocks, erasing his tracks as well as he could on the way out.

Then, the bottom half of him coated with stinking, drying slime, he began to climb to the trail. His horse stood there alone, reins dangling, and Shelter stepped into leather, riding back to join the army.

"Where have you been?" Realto demanded when he caught up with the general on the right-hand trail leading into the high country.

"I was trying to get the damned thing out," Shell said, indicating his filthy clothing. "Gato didn't seem to think it was worth trying very hard."

"No luck, I take it."

"No, not alone. I went back up to get my horse, thinking just maybe I could get it up and find a way out farther down—when I got back, Realto, the caisson had been stripped."

"Stripped!"

"The ammunition and dynamite has been taken. Gato

85

was in such a hurry to get back and tell you that the job was impossible that he left it behind. Now we got a problem," Shell said, looking away to the grassy hills ahead of the slowly marching army.

"What do you mean?"

"I mean," Morgan said, "someone's got that dynamite, and it's not us. This Tamaulipa war of ours might turn out to be something other than a little casual fun."

"Why they don't . . . they couldn't use that dynamite! How would they know what it was?"

"I hope you're right, Realto. A little dynamite can do terrible things to a human body. Arms and legs flying all over the place."

Realto blanched. "Damn Gato!"

"Yes, it kind of makes you wonder what he's up to, doesn't it? Choosing the wrong road, losing that gatling gun, leaving the dynamite for the Indians. Yes, sir, it kind of makes a man wonder."

Realto didn't answer. His thoughts were elsewhere, perhaps worrying that his men could very well find themselves attacked with explosives.

That was just what Shelter Morgan was thinking himself.

8.

On the grassy knoll in the shadow of the high peaks, night came early. The wind was cool and Morgan could hear it rustling the palm fronds in the jungle below, like surf lapping at the foot of the mountains.

He lay on his back beneath a single blanket, staring at the starry sky. It was time.

He had pushed things here about as far as he could. Gato was ready and eager to kill him, Realto was unsure. When they did encounter Tamaulipas it would become obvious that Morgan had no intention of cutting them down with a gatling gun just so that Villa's gunners could get some practice in.

It was time things were brought to a head, time Morgan stepped out of his role as Jim Pike and brought the war to Villa. He could very easily hang on longer, return to Villa's fortress and with time, find a way to eliminate Villa and Zack Willits both. With time—and in the meanwhile Villa's army would be moving across the country like deadly locusts, cutting down all in their path.

And so he had decided—it was time to make war.

After midnight he slipped from his bed and made his way to the caisson where the second gatling gun sat. No one was around. The perimeter guards were out quite a distance. The rest of the camp, exhausted from the day's march, slept soundly.

Morgan crouched beside the wheel of the caisson, eyes searching the camp. While he was down there he scooped up a double handful of mud. Then he climbed onto the caisson, keeping low, not wanting his silhouette against the starry background.

He placed his mud down and searched the gatling kit until he found the cleaning rod. Then he settled in to work. Mud was inserted in each barrel, then tamped down hard with the cleaning rod.

When he was through with that he wiped the barrels clean with a cloth from the kit, stowed the rod and rag away and slipped to the ground again.

Crossing toward the horses he nearly walked into the guard.

The man separated himself from the shadows and stood before Shelter. Shell saw the whiskered jaw, the face hidden in the shadow of his hat, the glint of star-light on his blued rifle all in a fraction of a second.

The rifle started to come up and Shelter Morgan moved. His hand went to the bowie knife at his hip and he lunged, his chest colliding with that of the guard and they went down together. Morgan's knife came up savagely, entering the throat of the Mexican just above the collar bone, severing windpipe and jugular.

The body convulsed beneath Shelter's hands. He could feel hot blood pumping onto the hand which was locked over the guard's mouth. After a minute there was no more movement, no more blood. He rose and moved on, dragging the guard behind him.

He rolled him into the rocks at the edge of the clearing, throwing his rifle after him. Then, wiping the cold sweat from his forehead, Shelter went to the horses.

The gray lifted its head in recognition and Shelter led it out of the string, leaving the tether loose. He chose a second mount and then started the horses walking.

Realto's men would lose a little time rounding them up. Not much, perhaps, but maybe enough to make a difference.

Leading his gray and a second horse into the trees he tied them loosely and returned to the camp. He knew where Mando was sleeping—he had tried to talk to him earlier in the evening. It hadn't been real successful. This time there wasn't going to be any conversation.

Morgan moved among the sleeping men, holding his breath as one soldier sat up, grumbling, flopped back down and began to snore loudly.

In another minute he was crouched over Mando, grateful for the antipathy of the other soldiers which kept Mando at a distance. There was no one nearer than fifty feet to where the kid slept.

"Sorry, Mando," Shelter said under his breath. Then he drew his Colt and thunked the barrel down behind the sleeping kid's ear. Mando trembled momentarily and then lapsed into a much deeper sleep.

In seconds Morgan had Mando across his shoulder and was creeping back across the camp, keeping to the perimeter where the trees kept him from outlining himself.

Again he stumbled onto a guard. This one was sitting on the ground, legs crossed, head bowed, rifle across his lap. He was sound asleep. He wouldn't be lasting long in Indian country, Shell decided.

He detoured around the guard and made it to where the horses stood hidden. He tossed Mando across the saddle, removed the kid's belt and lashed one wrist to one ankle beneath the horse's belly.

Then, stepping into the stirrup, he swung aboard the gray and began moving soundlessly off down the jungle clad slopes.

Daybreak found them at the big river. Sunlight glinted on its surface, silvering it. Parrots called from the jungle. Mando moaned again and sat up on the ground, holding his head. He looked around without seeing for a minute, then his eyes came into sharp focus, fixing on Shelter Morgan who sat facing him.

"You! What has happened? Where am I? Jim Pike! What is this? Where is everyone?"

Then he bowed his head again, holding it. After a minute he peered up through his fingers at Shell.

"You knocked me on the head and brought me here."

"That's right."

"But why?" Mando, confused and hurting, looked ready to cry.

"Take a guess," the bearded, one-eyed man said.

"You did not want me to fight with Villa's army—you are not on Villa's side," he said with sudden understanding, "you are his enemy!"

"That's right, Mando. Exactly right." Morgan pulled off his eye patch and Mando gaped. "I'm against him because he's murdering slime. He's a glory-hungry madman who doesn't care who gets killed as long as he gets wealthy and powerful. His 'people's revolution' is so much bullshit. He doesn't give a damn about the people, about boys like you."

"I do not believe you, Mister Pike. What you have done is wrong!"

"Maybe. But maybe one day you'll thank me for it."

"Thank you!" Mando shouted and he winced as his

90

head protested. "I curse you for it—and I am going back. There's nothing you can do to stop me."

"Oh, I won't stop you, kid." Shelter leaned back on one elbow, plucking a blade of grass. "But I sure wouldn't recommend going back. Not now."

"What do you mean?" Mando asked miserably.

"What I mean is there's a man dead back there. Everyone knows you came riding in with me, everyone knows you rode out with me last night. What sort of a reception do you think you'll get if you go riding back now? I think you know as well as I do—a bullet in the head."

"I will explain!"

"Think they'll listen, Mando? Those men? I know they won't, kid. That's why I brought you down to the river. There's a horse, there's the trail we came down on. I think you'll find a man can travel the other way on it. If you're in such a hurry to murder innocent people, why you just take yourself home and do it."

Mando's face was flaming. He started to protest that he was no murderer, started to curse Shelter Morgan for what he had done, but in the end he gave it up and just sat there, deflated and empty.

"I will go. What else can I do," he said finally. "But I will never forgive you for this, Pike. Never."

"I wouldn't expect you would—but don't lose any sleep over it. I won't. Now," Shelter said, rising, "I expect you'd better get going. There's a chance they'll try to track us down."

"You are not riding with me."

"No—don't worry about that. You're on your own now, and good luck to you. Me," he lifted his eyes to the mountain slopes, "I'm going back. I have to."

Mando just stared at him for a long time, not understanding the tall, blue-eyed gringo at all. Looking small, dejected, painfully unhappy, Mando Sandoval got onto his horse's back and rode out across the silver river, never looking back at Shelter Morgan.

Shell saddled up, slipped the bit into the reluctant gray's mouth, stepped into leather and rode out, chewing on salt biscuits from his saddlebags.

That was done with—Mando was gone. Now came the rest of it. The warring, the blood. And he was going to make war alone. Every man on that mountain stood against him. Every single human being was his enemy. It was a tall order and for a moment Morgan almost wished himself back on that trail, heading out of the jungle like Mando Sandoval.

A series of images kept running through his mind, banishing all thought of retreat. Villa raging, Bonita Madrid's dark, brave eyes, Zack Willits behind the sights of his rifle firing point-blank at Welton Williams long ago, far away, on another battlefield.

Morgan had to push thoughts of failure, or retreat out of his mind and concentrate on victory, on attack. Ahead lay the battlefield, ahead the enemy. And for some, bloody death.

He swung far to the west, circling the big, volcanic peak. There were no ancient trails on this side of the mountain, only dense jungle through which Shell had to pick his way carefully. From time to time there were broad lava fields, the black glassy rock sharp enough to cut a horse's hoofs to ribbons and dozens of times Morgan had to detour. Still by sunset he was high on the mountain, far to the south. If Realto hadn't given it up and turned back, Shelter should now be above them, directly in their path, his presence completely unexpected.

He stepped down from his horse wearily on a sheltered, barren outcropping which projected from the side of the big hill. Peering downward in the dusky light he could see no movement in the valleys below. Had Realto gone back?

The idea seemed absurd. He would have to push on and make his war. He could hardly return to Villa, report the loss of their training expert, Jim Pike, the loss of a gatling gun and a crate of dynamite and their failure to make enemy contact. Villa would explode with rage.

No, Realto would be coming on. He was down there now, in one of the dusk-shadowed valleys, sweltering, swearing, frustrated.

Shelter planned on seeing that the general was frustrated a hell of a lot more.

He unsaddled and sat for a time staring out across the empty land. There were still a few crimson banners against the sundown sky. After another minute the red lights below began to go on, and Shelter smiled. Realto's campfires pinpointed the enemy for him.

They were too far away for Shell to do anything on this night even and he wanted to. He didn't. What he wanted, needed more than anything else was a good night's rest. Realto was bogged down in the jungle and would be for a good long time yet. There was no hurry, no hurry at all.

Shelter, not lighting a fire of his own, rolled up in his blanket and slept.

When he awoke it was due to the persistent jabbing of something sharp and cold against his throat. He opened his eyes to the dawn sky, to see the tattooed Indian standing over him, his spear clenched in strong bronzed hands, the spearpoint hooked beneath Shelter's jaw.

Morgan didn't move, didn't twitch. He just stared at the Indian who was tattooed face and arms, legs and belly. He wore only a loincloth made from some primitively woven cloth. His hair was tied up in a topknot, decorated with what appeared to be polished bones.

His eyes were dark and savage and as he spoke to someone invisible to Shell, Morgan saw that his teeth were filed to points.

The others came forward now, three warriors, one of them already an old man, his leathery skin hanging from sinewy arms. His wrinkled, tattooed face hung over Morgan for a minute and he spoke to the man with the spear. What he said, Morgan had no idea, but the other one responded violently. The old man repeated his words calmly and then walked away.

The Tamaulipa with the spear jabbed again and Shell felt a thin trickle of hot blood begin to run down his throat.

Then, as with disgust he turned away. Three more Indians swarmed over Shelter, lifting his Colt and belt knife, his Winchester.

He was yanked to his feet and his hands were tied behind his back with rough rope. One of them took his horse and rode off toward the jungle, leaving the saddle behind.

Someone grunted something at Shell and he was prodded roughly in the back, hurried into the jungle at a dog trot, the Tamaulipas surrounding him.

So much for the war. So much for getting Zack Willits, stopping Hector Villa. So much for everything. Whatever these bastards had in mind, it wasn't Southern hospitality. Maybe they liked to torture a man first, skin him alive or tie him down to one of those jungle anthills, slit off his eyelids and tie him looking at the sun.

Shelter fell, banged a knee roughly and was jerked to his feet. He ran on, following the lead Tamaulipa along the narrow jungle trail which wove uphill and down, through vine-hung trees and barren stretches of lava and ash.

The sun glinted through the trees. There was no sound but the thudding of feet against the earth, the hammering in Shelter's skull.

They followed a trail no more than eighteen inches wide along the side of the mountain where the drop-off to the rocks below was two thousand feet or more. The Tamaulipas didn't slow down a bit and so Morgan didn't. He plodded on, his legs growing heavy, his feet in Western boots growing cramped and hot.

He fell again and again they picked him up, their faces expressionless, and again they ran.

By mid-morning they were nearly to the top of the volcano. Here for some reason the trees began again and grass grew. They passed several narrow creeks burbling down through the black rocks.

Suddenly they were in the village. Naked brown kids and dogs, yapping at their heels appeared everywhere. Old women with tattoos on their faces peered out of palm-frond shacks.

There was a lot of shouting and a few rocks were winged at Morgan, one of them catching his shoulder painfully. Suddenly everyone fell away. They were among the trees again, great glossy-leaved trees like none Shelter had ever seen before.

95

And there was a stockade. It was built of sharpened stakes driven into the ground, bound together with some sort of crude hemp. Shelter was pushed inside and the door shut behind him.

For a time he could see the curious faces peering in through the spaces between the stakes. Then, as the sun began its descent, they drifted away. From the village Shell could hear the sound of log drums being beaten. He could see the wavering reddish light of a fire, see the two sentries slowly walking around the stockade, their spears in hand, and he lay back exhausted, dazed, soaking in the hopelessness of his situation.

He was completely at their mercy. He couldn't see any way out of the stockade, any way of overpowering the watching Indians. Even if he could somehow accomplish that, he wasn't going to make it far before they ran him down. Not down that mountain slope, afoot.

Still his mind was active, for the man who gives up is the man who loses. He noted a short, jagged stick lying in one corner of the stockade, counted the number of steps the sentries took, how long their round was, knowing all the while that it was futile. They had him, they would keep him as long as they wanted to. They identified him with Villa's men, the men who came killing in their jungle, and Morgan knew they would have no mercy.

9.

The morning sun was a dazzling assault upon the eyes and Shelter held his hand in front of his face as he squinted up at the four dark figures standing before him. One of them he recognized—the big one with the spear, the one who had wanted to kill him immediately.

They spoke among themselves in their own tongue then switched to Spanish: "Come with us now."

Shelter rose a little stiffly and was led out of the compound. They walked back through the village, veered right toward the volcano's peak and entered dense jungle again. Beside the trail, Shelter noticed, was a carved stone monument like those he had seen below.

Birds called loudly in the sun-bright jungle. Shelter's spirits were higher than they had been the night before— they weren't ready to kill him out of hand. There would be some talking first, and that meant there was a chance. It was only when the talking ended that the killing started.

They emerged into a clearing where long, trampled-down grass grew. Ahead was a thatched hut, larger than any he had seen before.

A carved wooden mask, fierce and toothy hung over the entranceway. Shelter was taken to the hut and shown inside.

He sat there on a straw mat, a man as old as the mountain, every inch of his body covered with tattoos, a bone necklace hanging down his shrunken chest, bone earrings dangling from the long lobes of his ears.

Two hands were placed on Morgan's shoulders and he was forceably seated. The old man just sat there, his eyes on Shell, but distant, smoky. A shadow fell across the floor of the hut as someone else entered. Morgan's head swiveled slightly then jerked up.

He couldn't help staring. She was young, bronzed, lovely. Glossy black hair fell down her back to her waist. She wore only a cotton skirt wrapped around her waist and knotted there. Her breasts were bare, full, dark-nippled and completely agreeable.

The expression on her beautiful, flat-cheeked face was not. She said something to one of the warriors then sat beside the old man, facing Morgan.

"Are you Villa?" she said suddenly in explosive Spanish, her eyes cutting at Morgan.

"No." He had to smile and the girl didn't like it. She spoke to the old man, apparently translating.

"You are with Villa?"

"No."

"Who are you?" she demanded.

"I am Villa's enemy. I've come here to destroy him," Morgan said, keeping his voice even, his eyes on those of the young woman.

The tall man with the spear interrupted vehemently. He stepped forward and shook a fist at Shell. The girl snapped at him and he stepped back, still scowling, rubbing a tattooed arm.

"Kaska says you are a lying man," the girl said. "He wants to cut your bowels out," she added casually.

"I'm not lying."

"He says you only seek to save your life. What other reason would you have for being in our land?"

"I've explained that."

"You are here to destroy Villa."

"That's right."

The girl's eyes narrowed. She pursed her lips thoughtfully. "You speak Spanish incorrectly."

"I'm not Mexican," Shell answered.

"North American."

"Yes."

"I have heard of that place," she said. The warrior erupted again, pointing at Shelter, spreading his arms as he gestured to the girl who turned and explained something to the old man who grunted one word and lifted a finger. The warrior fell back in silence.

"Tahapo says you must be heard." The woman inclined her head toward the withered old man.

"Tahapo is your chief?"

"Tahapo is chief."

"And who are you?"

"I am called Matin. I am Tahapo's daughter."

Tahapo said something in his dry, cracked voice. The girl translated. "My father wishes to know this—how are you going to destroy Villa. You are one man alone."

"I will destroy Villa because he is wrong," Morgan said. "I will destroy him because he is evil. Because he is a fool."

"My father has not asked this. He has asked you how you will do it."

"With your help," Morgan said, snatching the idea out of the blue.

The tall warrior, Kaska, began to rant again. Shelter

99

had the idea they weren't going to get along too well. He had always had trouble making friends with people who wanted to disembowel him.

"What do you mean?" the girl asked warily.

"Just this," Shell said, the idea taking its own inertia, "I am Villa's enemy and I have come here to stop him from making bloody war. I know he wishes to fight the Tamaulipas with new and terrible weapons. I can't fight him myself no matter how much of a warrior I am," Shell was leaning forward intently, gesturing with his hands, "but I knew that the Tamaulipas are a fierce, proud people with brave warriors among them. I knew that they are the equal to Villa's men—except they do not have these new weapons which Villa possesses."

"And you have?" Kaska demanded.

Shelter half turned around to answer the Indian. "Yes, I have these weapons."

"You would use them against Villa?"

"That's why I got them."

"And you wish to fight with us—that is the reason you came to our jungle?"

"That is correct."

"I do not believe any of this!" Kaska shouted. No, he didn't. His eyes were black, scathing as he hovered over Shelter, his chest heaving with emotion. "This enemy has been captured on our land. He has come among us to spy. He is white—not Spanish, but white. Why would he wish to help us?"

"Why, stranger?" the girl asked.

"My name is Shelter Morgan," he answered with a smile. "I came to fight Villa, not necessarily to help you, though I'm happy if it works out that way. I am white, you are Indian. Villa and most of his men are some of

100

each. Race doesn't have anything to do with being good, honorable or just. I will also tell you this—Villa has men with him who are my blood enemies. North Americans as I am. Long ago they killed the men in my war party, slaughtered them. They were supposed to be friends of ours. They were not. I must avenge my friends' deaths."

Matin translated that for the old man who nodded heavily—that sort of motive he could understand.

"This man thinks he has strong magic," Kaska said disparagingly. "Enough magic to beat the man Villa."

"I have it," Shelter said, his face sober and set. "With your help I have enough magic and enough knowledge to defeat this man who would throw you out of your homes and murder you."

Kaska just snorted. The old man waited while his daughter finished translating, then shrugged, answering her rapidly. Kaska cried out in protest.

"My father says that it may be so that you have brought magic to us."

"We must kill him," Kaska interrupted. Matin shot him a hard glance and went on.

"My father says that it may be you are the enemy of Villa. We must give you a chance to prove yourself."

"No. He must be killed!"

"And then," the girl said, "if you fail, you will be killed. Do you understand?"

"Perfectly," Morgan said.

"Then," she shrugged, lifting one smooth brown shoulder, "so it will be, Shelter Morgan."

With that she gestured for him to rise and went out into the sunlight which beamed down through a gap in the trees. Kaska was right at his shoulder.

"If this is a trick, Shelter Morgan, you will die. Very

101

painfully, not all at once. Do you understand me?"

"Yes, I understand."

"You are not afraid?"

"Why should I be? It's not a trick. I told you nothing but the truth. Together you and I will defeat Villa—you shall see."

Kaska wasn't so easily placated. He turned his head and spat, glared again at Shelter and called his men to him. "For now you are a prisoner still, Shelter Morgan. These men will take you back to your stockade."

And they did, grabbing an arm and turning him, walking him soundlessly down the slope. Morgan had only a last fleeting glimpse of a copper-skinned, dark eyed girl standing in the entranceway of the hut watching after him.

The village was deserted but for the dogs, the very young and the very old. Everyone else seemed to be out working, gathering roots and berries, perhaps.

The stockade was empty too. They shoved Morgan in, closed the gate and resumed their vigil while he sat in the ribbon of shade cast by the stockade wall, knees drawn up, wondering just what in hell he was doing this far from home among a bunch of savage Indians, planning a war against a well-equipped army. His magic, he decided, had better be damned strong.

The day passed slowly, the shade creeping across the ground before Shell's eyes. A large beast called out in the jungle and its roar echoed up the mountain slope.

The girl came an hour before sunset.

She was frowning as she entered. Shelter got a quick glimpse of the two guards behind her. She came near to him and crouched down. Shelter let his eyes caress her smooth, full breasts and she gazed at him wonderingly.

"What is it?"

"You're very beautiful, Matin."

"Of course," she answered simply. "What are you doing here, in the stockade?"

"This is where Kaska brought me."

She made a sharp, dissatisfied sound. "Kaska can be a fool. You are not a prisoner any longer. You are a warrior. A hut will be found for you. First—" She beckoned and a stout, older woman appeared, carrying a straw basket.

"What is that?"

"Food. You must eat."

Shelter's stomach tightened anxiously. It had been a while since he had eaten. "Then," she said, "you must purify yourself for the battle. You have no woman so I will help you."

"Purify myself?"

"Clean the body so that the spirit is clean and strong."

He nodded, figuring he could use a bath all right. The food was pasty, nearly tasteless. He thought it was plantain, but couldn't be sure. He filled his belly with it anyway.

"Who is Kaska?" he asked as he ate.

"Kaska is war leader."

"So he doesn't like me because I'll make war plans and not him?"

"Kaska does not like whites. He does not like anyone very much, I think."

"How about you, Matin?" Shell asked. "Does he like you?"

"Oh, yes. Kaska likes me. He likes me very much—I will be his wife when this war is over." She said it with distaste. Morgan pushed the basket aside and rose. The sun was already behind the mountain peak and the land was deep in shadows.

"I'd like that bath now."

"Yes, come along."

She led him out of the stockade, the guards there watching with mixed emotions. Presumably they were going to catch hell from Kaska, yet none of them dared to tell the chief's daughter what she could or could not do.

Matin led off through the close forest. There were dense fern, some waist high and vines climbing the trunks of the trees. There was a soft orange, sundown glow to the sky and a soft, almost whispering breeze moving through the jungle.

They came suddenly upon a rocky basin where water stood clear and cold. From above a trickle of a stream fed the pond.

"You must bathe," she told Shell.

He looked at her, wondering if she wasn't going to leave, but she stood, hands clasped before her, her bare breasts softly rising and falling as she hummed a tuneless song.

Morgan shrugged and stripped his shirt off, sat down and tugged off his boots. Matin still watched with idle curiosity. Shell stood, took off his pants and stepped naked into the dark, silent pool.

Still Matin only watched, standing almost prayerfully above him, a dark figure against the darker trees as night began to fall.

Shell scrubbed up as well as possible, ducking under the cold water to soak his hair. Then he rose and walked out into the night.

Matin was there and she looked him up and down with curiosity. Morgan dressed and still she watched.

"Now, come with me," she said as if he were a child, and he followed along. She went upslope through the tangle of jungle vegetation there. It was nearly full dark and Shell had to stay close or lose her.

They were suddenly at a tiny hut sitting alone on a narrow ledge. Matin was waiting for him. He stopped, catching his breath, looking out at the empty night as the stars twinkled on. There were other lights, far distant. Soft red, glowing against the darkness of the land.

"Our enemies," Matin said, standing beside Shelter, staring at Realto's campfires. "You must be cleansed, you must be strong so that you may vanquish our enemies, Shelter Morgan.

She went then into the little hut, Shelter followed, ducking to clear the low lintel. He couldn't see anything at first. He could smell it, however. It was pungent, heavily scented with herbs or fragrant plants. He saw a spark in the darkness, then Matin bending low over a fire ring, puffing a flame to life as she added tinder.

Now he knew what Tamaulipa women wore under their bark skirts. Nothing at all. Morgan smiled, watching the intent expression on the woman's face, her breasts hanging pendulous, her sleek dark hair, the line of her back, and from directly behind the twin smooth globes of her honey-toned buttocks, the dark mysterious line between them.

The fire was going and now Matin rose, wiping back her hair. Her eyebrows drew together as she looked at Shell and found him smiling.

She went to the corner then and brought out a gourd and a dipper. There was water in the gourd and she splashed some onto the fire, raising a cloud of steam. One of the rocks cracked loudly.

Bustling around, Matin returned with a bowl filled with something yellow, pungent, a clean cloth, a sack full of herbs or some such which she tossed onto the fire, scenting the steam which still rose from the fire.

"Undress, please again," she said in a businesslike way and Shelter at first did nothing. "Did you hear me? We must have you purified for battle."

Morgan began undressing again and as he did Matin continued to sprinkle water on the stones, sift herbs over the fire and sway to the rhythm of her distant humming.

He stood there naked, towering over her. Outside it was dark and silent. In here it was warm. The steam was soothing. There was a vaguely pleasant sensation in inhaling the herbal scent.

"Now," she said, rising suddenly, looking Morgan up and down appraisingly, "let us see. Yes, you have the fine body of a warrior—very strong, I think."

Then without another word she stepped out of her skirt. One moment it was on, the next it lay against the floor, and Matin knelt down at Shelter's feet, pulling the bowl to her.

She began then to soap him down with the yellow cream from the bowl, her hands running up his calves then his thighs, her hands working the soap into the great muscles there.

Shelter just closed his eyes. The steam seemed to be cleansing, taking over his body, inducing a dreamy warmth. He tried to think of other things, but it was impossible and he gave it up. Slowly his erection rose as Matin, still kneeling in front of him, soaped his hard buttocks, her breasts bumping softly against his legs.

Her fingers were magical, pleasing and knowing. She

106

took his erection and soaped it quickly, doing the same for his sack. Shelter looked down at her, but there was nothing erotic in the way she studied him as she worked.

Her eyes were far distant, her humming continued. She stood and did his chest, her hands working in small circular patterns. Then she slipped behind him and did his back.

"Down, please," she said and Shell complied. He sat on the mat while she soaped his hair, her pelvis, softly downed with coal black hair, nudging his shoulder. The steam continued to billow up. Morgan was aware now of perspiration rolling off his body.

Matin had finished with the soap. Now she picked up the gourd pitcher and began to run clear water over him, rinsing his hair, her strong hands working through it then down to his neck where she paused to exert pressure with her fingertips, working the soreness out of his knotted muscles.

She was close against him, her breasts grazing his back tantalizingly.

"Up," she said and he stood, feeling weak, telling himself it was the steam.

She worked her way on down with the same expertise, the same quick, casual rinsing of his sex organs. She was to his feet then and Shell watched as she bent low, her buttocks uptilted, her head bowing as she kissed his feet, astonishing him.

He put his hand on her head, bending low to touch her. Matin rose quickly, walking to the corner, returning with a cloth which was also scented. She began to rub Shelter down. She rubbed until his skin glowed and her own face was streaked with perspiration from the effort.

"Now," she said, finally satisfied, "you are purified. And now—" she allowed herself a smile. "You may give the pledge."

"The what?" Shelter asked and then he didn't have to. Matin stepped in close and her hands encircled his erection. She rubbed the head of the shaft briefly against her smooth belly then kissed his chest. She stepped back and looked down at the warm living thing she held in her hands, her eyes glowing. She cupped his sack and exhaled sharply through her teeth.

"I will tell you," she said, her fingers running up and down his length, "about the pledge. It is the way of our people. There is a battle to be fought now; always there have been battles. Many men go off to fight but they do not all return, Shelter Morgan . . ."

She had a little trouble speaking for a moment. She had spread her legs and lifted herself on tiptoes. Now she touched the head of his erection to her damp inner flesh, rubbing it gently back and forth. Shell could see her legs begin to tremble.

"The pledge," he reminded her.

"When a man goes away he may not come back. Then there are only the women. If there are no babies in their wombs then there will be no more Tamaulipas when the men are killed. There must always be a Tamaulipa people and so the night before battle the men must take the warriors' pledge, they must fill their woman's womb with hot seed and promise that they have made a child, a man-child who will grow up to be a warrior to replace his father."

"Interesting custom," Shelter managed to say. His throat was dry and constricted. Matin knelt again. Her cheek was against his thigh, her eyes lifted to him, bright

108

and sparkling.

"It is," she said breathily, "necessary. It is the ritual, it is the way things are done. You have no woman, and since you must lead us in battle, I have come to take your pledge."

He gave it to her gladly.

10.

Matin was on her knees before him. Steam clouded the small hut in the Tamaulipa village. Her lips met his inner thigh, worked around to his buttocks and traced the line between them up his spine. She took his fingers and drew him after her to a far corner where a mattress had been placed.

As Shell watched, Matin got down on her back, running hands across her breasts, her fingers toying with the taut dark nipples. Then, with a little shudder she raised her knees and her fingers went between her legs, parting the dark pubic down giving him a glimpse of what lay beyond.

He got to his knees and kissed her soft, flat belly, her thighs, smelling the musky, exciting scent of her. Her hand flicked out and grasped his shaft, her thumb running across the head of it as he kissed her from toe to eyebrow.

Slowly, lazily, Matin rolled onto her belly and lifted her rear end. Her head was turned to one side, veiled with dark hair, her hand was a trembling, grasping thing and Shelter slid up behind her, feeling her anxious finger position him.

Then he slid into her deep, incredible warmth, his hands resting on her perspiration-glossed ass which twitched beneath the honey-colored smooth flesh.

110

She drew him in farther, her hand reaching back far between her own legs to find his sack and press it against her as if she would take it into her as well.

She held perfectly still for a moment, only the awakening inner muscles of her body moving, caressing him, encouraging the release of the pledge.

Slowly her body seemed to come to tremulous life. He felt the slow thrusting of her hips, the side to side swaying increase in tempo. Shelter glanced down, saw himself where he entered Matin, saw her fingers around him.

Suddenly she lifted her head, her neck arched and her body slammed against him, devouring him, her buttocks pounding against his pelvis as she wriggled furiously, almost desperately, her demanding rhythm building to a crazed tempo.

Still she was humming, or Morgan thought at first that she was. Then he recognized the low, animal mewing in her throat for what it was. She was coming undone inside, and the thought of that excited him still more.

He fairly lifted her from the ground as he slammed against her, raising her higher and higher until her legs unfolded and locked around his waist.

Morgan reached a sudden hard climax. He fell against her, his hands reaching around to clutch at Matin's glorious breasts. And still she moved against him, whimpering softly, a tear running down across her smooth cheek.

Barely breaking rhythm Shelter rolled her onto her back, seeing her misted, far seeing eyes fixed on his face, seeing the pleasure blossom there with each deep, slow stroke. Her hands slid up behind him and clenched his buttocks, one finger trailing into the crack as she spread her legs and thrust them high into the air.

111

She bit down on her lip as Shelter bent his mouth to her breasts, taking in one nipple and then the other, his hands clutching at her shoulders, then slipping down lower to lift her, to press him against her as he rocked against Matin's sweat-slick, quivering body building to a second climax as her mouth dropped open and a muffled cry from deep within her split the silence.

It was cool, the moon screened behind the trees glowing dully and Shelter awoke with Matin beside him. He awoke suddenly from out of a deep, deep sleep. He sat up in the darkness, his heart hammering away.

He walked to where his clothes were stacked and pulled on his pants, creeping toward the door to the hut. He looked cautiously out, seeing nothing, hearing nothing.

But there had been something. Someone come a-peeping. That had awakened him, his warrior's instincts reacting to some faint sound which could only be made by a man.

Now there was nothing, only the wide-leafed jungle trees highlighted by the moonlight, the softly sleeping girl behind him.

"Kaska," he told himself. "He knows and he won't like it a bit."

It would complicate things a bit, and Shelter didn't like it. It was hard enough to face the enemy without having to worry about the men in your own ranks. Shelter touched his throat, feeling the drying scab there. Then, shaking it off, he finished dressing.

The morning brought a haze drifting in off of the Gulf, blanketing the lower elevations in gray mist. On the volcano it was startlingly clear, already warm.

Shelter had been given his horse and his guns. Someone had gone back to fetch his saddle. The gray stood

112

waiting patiently beside Tahapo's hut where the war leaders were meeting. It was time to fight.

"I think," Shelter was telling them, "it might be a good idea to unnerve them a little first. If we could have a few men with darts work along their flanks firing and then retreating silently . . ."

"We must go at them, attack, attack!" Kaska interrupted.

"Let the man speak, Kaska," Tahapo said, his old face infinitely patient.

"Thank you. The use of darts brings silent death. When men begin to fall out of ranks, silently killed as if the jungle itself were reaching out hands and killing them, the others will become uncertain. They will look around anxiously, not knowing where death will strike next."

Matin sat to one side, looking sleek and satisfied. Shelter smiled at her.

"There will come a time when we must fight face to face," Kaska said. "If we do not they will eventually reach our village and destroy all, perhaps kill the women and children."

"Yes," Morgan agreed, "there will come a time. But we will use the time the silent harassment can buy us to prepare for the confrontation."

"How do you mean, Shelter Morgan?" one of the other war leaders asked.

"I have hidden weapons which we can use against the invader. Explosives. A gun which fires many times without needing to be reloaded."

"So you say," Kaska muttered. "I do not like this. I do not like you. Tahapo believes your magic is good, that you were sent to lead us into battle. I believe you are a liar

113

and a trickster!"

"You're wrong, Kaska," Shell answered evenly, "and I mean to prove it to you."

"You shall," Kaska hissed. "I shall see that you do prove it, Shelter Morgan."

The man's eyes were overflowing with hatred, his mouth set with tight menace. The old chief began to speak now and Shelter waited while Matin translated.

"My father says," she began quietly, worriedly, "that you must understand this, Shelter Morgan. He is trusting you. He is hoping that you have good magic, that you are a war leader for the Tamaulipas. But you must understand that if you are anything else you will be given over to Kaska and very slowly, very painfully killed."

Shelter nodded. Kaska had brightened a little. He wanted blood, but not just any blood. It was Morgan's he craved.

"I understand this," Shell said, lifting his blue eyes to meet Tahapo's. "I would have it no other way."

He rose suddenly and Kaska flinched. Shelter smiled thinly. "Let's make us a war, Kaska. You are my enemy now—but we have a common cause. For now, let's forget our personal war."

"For now," Kaska answered, and Morgan knew that was all he could hope for. When the war was over then it would be Kaska's turn.

Outside Shell mounted, looking down at the sea of mist. Somewhere Realto and Gato Hernandez led their army toward this camp. Somewhere in the distance a mad man sat comfortably at his table, indulging his body while a young woman was held captive and the war drums sounded in the jungle.

"It's time," Shell said to Kaska who stood beside him

114

tattooed and menacing. Morgan looked over the fifty Tamaulipas who had gathered around him—his army. Then he nodded, heeled the gray and started back down the mountain, a runner out ahead of them to act as scout, Kaska close behind him, the deadly spear clenched tightly in his hand.

An hour later they were in the mist themselves. Warm, sultry it hung from the trees like gray cobwebs. It reminded Shelter of last night and the steam—of course almost everything reminded him of last night with Matin. There was no time for such indulgence, however, and he forced himself to become what he was—a soldier preparing for battle.

The runner came in as Shelter and his Indian warriors forded a thin, quick running rill and prepared to climb the slope opposite. He had run a long ways, but there was no exhaustion on his face, only elation.

"Half a mile on," he reported to Kaska.

"Now we attack and drive them from the jungle!" Kaska said, lifting his arms. His men cheered but Shelter, surveying them from horseback said loudly:

"No! You all know what the battle plan is. We aren't going to face them head-on. Not just yet."

"Are you frightened, Morgan? Or is it that you want to prevent us from killing your friends?"

"Neither," Morgan answered calmly. "It is that I want to win this war, and charging at them with spears is not the way to do it. They'll cut us down."

"He is right, Kaska," one of the warriors said. A tall man who carried himself with dignity, he looked at Morgan then shrugged. "The man is right."

"You are a fool, Itza. Why do you trust this man over me? Why do you wish to follow him?"

"Because," Itza said, "it is what Tahapo has told us we must do."

"Itza is right," someone said.

"Tahapo has told us we must follow this man."

Kaska was enraged, but holding his anger back. "Very well," he said. "Do not blame me if this comes to tragedy." He turned his back on them all then and Shell studied him a moment, seeing the muscles of the warrior's back swollen with rage, the tendons on his neck standing taut. This one, Shell knew, wouldn't be happy until Morgan was carved into little pieces and the parts scattered across the jungle.

"Itza, we need to have four or five men with blowguns." Shell told them what to do. "Harass them from the flanks, then from the rear. Aim carefully, let your darts do the work. Then when they turn to search for you, be ghosts in the jungle. Kill silently and disappear."

Those warriors who did not speak Spanish stood in a circle, looking expectantly at Itza who turned and told them what must be done. Six men, all armed with blow-guns and poisoned darts loped off upslope, vanishing through the trees.

"Now," Morgan said in English, "let's have at it."

It took most of the morning to reach the spot where the gatling gun had been abandoned and a good hour to pull it from the muck and slime.

"Such a gun," Itza said, "but how can we use it? It is too large to carry in a battle."

"It is. Without the caisson. We'll take it back to the village and position it on the trail somewhere. It'll be the last line of defense. They'll never get past it, I promise you that."

116

"Who is to say this gun shoots?" Kaska asked scornfully.

Shelter grimaced. The Indian was getting to be a real pain in the ass. He would destroy his own people to get revenge on Shelter. It wasn't a bad idea to check it out, though and Morgan decided to do just that. He led them to where his ammunition and explosives were hidden and they toted the load back to where the gatling lay on its side.

"There's a metal frame on that caisson, Itza. Get it."

When the gatling was set up, Kaska still smirking stood right in front of it. "Shoot me, Morgan, show me how the gun kills."

"Get out of the way," Morgan growled. "You're not helping anyone by acting like this. If you think this ungainly looking weapon doesn't deal in death and destruction, my friend, you're wrong. There isn't anything like it in the world, and it'll be a long time before there's something better. As of now its the most efficient killing machine known to man. It's not something you play with. Now get the hell out of the way!"

Shelter jammed a clip down the gullet of the gatling, swung the barrel to the side and began to crank the handle.

She sang beautifully. A deep throated, staccato roar filled the jungle. The old lady lifted her deadly voice in song and the trunks of the trees along the clearing perimeter were blown to bark and splinters. The gatling chattered and several of the Tamaulipas broke and ran as the thunder of her death song rolled across the jungle and the hot, searching missiles flew from her many throats.

Smoke rose in a blue haze as Shelter finished the clip and stood behind the gatling, studying the faces of the

117

stunned Tamaulipas. Maybe Shelter wasn't a man of magic, but R.J. Gatling had produced a kind of magic the Indians understood and just now Shell was getting the credit for it.

"We are saved," one warrior said almost reverently. Another man moved in closer and touched the warm, still smoking cluster of barrels.

"Is there another such gun as this?" Itza asked.

"There's another. And it's close. Villa's men have one."

"What is this?" Kaska asked and Shell leaped toward him. The Tamaulipa had picked up a stick of dynamite. It wasn't fused, and dynamite is usually pretty stable, but Morgan recalled an old prospector in Denver telling him just how stable it was minutes before he blew himself up.

"Put that down!"

"Why? What is it?"

There was something in Kaska's eyes which made Shelter decide he didn't want to tell the Indian just what it was yet. A wise man always kept something in reserve.

"Leave it alone. It's not important," Morgan said and Kaska, shrugging, tossed the red stick back into the box.

The Indians built a sling out of thick vines and four of them headed off toward the village on the mountain with the gatling gun. Another man carried the ammunition and dynamite.

"Now," Morgan said, "let's have a closer look at the enemy."

They headed west by south, following narrow trails along the flanks of the hills, through the jungle-clotted low lands.

The mist persisted. It was a heavy, damp blanket across the world. When they came upon Realto's men it was so

118

sudden that Shelter yanked back roughly on the reins and the gray went up on hind legs. He stepped down, slapping the gray on the rump.

There he was. Marching slowly forward along a winding trail across a grassy expanse atop an isolated knoll.

The Mexicans saw them almost at the same time and men rushed forward, kneeling, rifles to their shoulders. Realto himself walked his side-stepping black horse to the point and sat looking at the motley band of Indians, the all too-recognizable tall man on the gray horse at their head.

They couldn't hear Realto's orders but they saw two riders take off for the rear of the column.

"What is happening?" Itza asked with a hint of nervousness in his voice.

"Watch."

He didn't have to wait long to have his question answered. The caisson came flying up from the rear of the column, the two horses drawing it feeling the lash of the excited driver. In the back a gunner clung to the gatling. Two outriders shouted excitedly to the foot soldiers who scurried out of the path of the racing caisson.

"Back into the trees," Itza said excitedly.

"No."

"Are you mad—you have shown us what those guns can do."

"Maybe it can do nothing against Shelter Morgan's magic," Kaska jeered. "Eh, Morgan?"

"Maybe not," Shelter said softly.

Realto's horse pranced across the front of the ranks. No one had ordered the soldiers into position, no one had

119

told them to load and fire and so they did nothing. They stood pointing at the Indians, talking among themselves.

The gatling-carrying caisson swung around to the front, kicking up dust, the wheel on the near side nearly lifting from the ground.

In seconds the horses were unhitched and led away and the gunner jammed a magazine into the breech of the gatling.

"Now, Morgan!" Itza said. "We must leave."

Kaska's face was dripping with sweat and it wasn't all from the oppressive humidity. "Go on if you want," Shelter told them.

"And you?" Kaska asked, his lip curling back.

"They can't hurt me—you should realize that."

"Magic!"

"Sure." Shelter lifted a shoulder as if it were of no importance.

"Now!" The command was Realto's and the Indians scattered as the gunner cranked down on the gatling. The explosion blew the gunner high into the air, smashed the caisson to kindling, knocked Realto from his horse and sent a dozen horses to running.

The gatling gun itself, Shelter saw as the smoke cleared, had peeled its barrels into strips of jagged metal.

"That mud do make it hard to fire one of those," Shelter said, shaking his head. He looked around. The Indians to a man were in the trees, peering out in amazement. Shell sauntered that way to join them before Realto came to his senses and ordered a rifle barrage.

Just now Villa's general was lying on the ground, watching his men try to pull his boot free of the stirrup.

Shell put on his best straight face and, finding Kaska said, "Let's get on up the mountain."

"What happened?"

"What do you think?"

"I do not think it was magic."

"All right." Shelter shrugged again and walked past the awed Indians to where his horse stood. He swung up and watched Kaska head off at a jog trot through the mist. He had time to cast one last cold scowl at Morgan. No, he didn't believe in any magic.

He didn't have to. He only had to believe that Morgan could lead them in this war. That, perhaps, he was starting to believe.

Shelter was thinking of something else. They were outnumbered and outgunned. Nothing could make Realto pull off after this incident. They needed an edge of some kind, needed it badly, and it wasn't going to do to sit waiting for the magic to return.

11.

The gatling gun had been carried to the village before Shelter made it back with his contingent. Three of the blow-gunners had returned. They claimed they had killed ten of Realto's men. But two of them had been cut down. The numbers weren't good. If they killed ten Villa men for every three of their own, it still wasn't enough. Shelter hoped the dead had made a good pledge with their women.

He saw Matin as he entered the camp, but he couldn't allow himself the luxury of thinking about her. There was still an hour or two of light left, and something had to be done about their defenses.

Pausing only long enough to take a drink of water from a gourd pitcher, Shelter led the way back down the trail, four men carrying the gatling, another toting the dynamite behind him.

He had seen the place he wanted the gun. The trail made a sharp inward hairpin half a mile from the camp. Above the trail was a ledge. Behind that was a shallow cave. A gun placed there would command the entire mountainside—as long as the ammunition lasted. There wasn't a lot of it. The rest, Morgan figured, had to be back in the shed at the Madrid house. Well, maybe he would be picking some up when he went back—because he *was* going back to the house Villa had captured. The Willits brothers were there, Villa himself.

And Bonita Madrid.

"Up there," Shelter told them.

"How?"

"Get some ropes. That hemp you use might be strong enough. Have a couple of your boys scramble up there. We'll tie on and hoist away."

"We should be attacking," Kaska grumbled, all the same he gave the orders to do as Morgan requested.

With Itza and the man carrying the dynamite, Shelter went farther down the trail, keeping his eyes turned up for handy outcroppings.

"I don't understand what you are doing," Itza said as Shell stood staring up at a likely shelf of black rock.

"This dynamite makes an explosion. Like a gun, only much bigger. Big enough to tear that rock down and cause it to fall on Villa's men."

"How does it know when they are coming?" Itza asked, obviously puzzled.

"Someone will have to be here. Look." Shelter opened a slat on the crate and removed a stick of dynamite. Reaching in he pulled out a coil of fuse. Shell hadn't done any mining for some time and he couldn't remember the color codes well enough to determine how fast that fuse was. He cut off six inches with his knife, fished a match out of his shirt pocket and thumbnailed it to life.

Itza watched as if some magical ceremony was going to take place. Shell touched the match to the fuse and watched it sizzle to life. He counted as it burned to the other end. It was fairly fast, probably best for this work.

"Nothing happened," a bewildered Itza said as the fuse burned out.

123

"It wasn't supposed to. Look, the fuse is placed like this. Then when the fire reaches the dynamite, boom!"

Itza grinned. Now he understood and he liked the idea. With Itza leading the way Morgan climbed up to have a look at that ledge. It was all volcanic rock, with a massive, jagged seam running through it. It was a dandy place to set a charge. Shell looked up, feeling the smooth black stone. Eight sticks or so, just to make sure, he decided.

The dynamite was tossed up and Morgan set the charge as Itza crouched, watching.

"Who will light this?"

"Someone will have to stay nearby. We'll run the fuse up over the rock there. Then whoever lights it can take off for the village along that ridge. He'll have to time it— say when he sees Villa's men round the first bend. Not that one, the first bend."

Itza nodded his understanding. Shell finished laying out the fuse and came down to the ledge again.

"Why are you doing this?" Itza asked.

Morgan was wiping his forehead. Now he put his hat back on and stood, hands on hips, breathing a little raggedly.

"I don't like Villa."

"That you have said; but Villa is not here. He is far away from our mountain."

"Let me put it another way then. I don't like Villa, I don't like his kind of people. I don't like someone having his own way just because he's got the biggest gun, and when I see it happening I generally take a hand. I found out a long while ago there's no point in waiting for someone else to come along and keep the thugs and outlaws off. Odds are just as good they'll join them."

"I understand."

"Good." It was fine—Shelter just wasn't so sure he understood it himself sometimes. He only knew that was the way things were. There's right and wrong in the world, and there's got to be somebody to help out the little people, those with the smaller guns—or like the Tamaulipas, with no guns at all.

They dragged back into camp at sundown. The place was very quiet and Itza told him why.

"The women and children have gone into the hills. There will be death nearby and we will not have it take them."

Shelter ate with Itza and the man who had carried the dynamite. They sat around a tiny fire eating boar meat and maize. When Morgan looked up he saw Matin standing across the fire, her body glossed with firelight. Smoky shadows moved across her bare breasts, her belly. Her eyes were lost in darkness.

"May I speak to you?" she asked.

"Sure." He rose, put his bowl down, took Matin's arm at the elbow and walked a little ways with her into the trees.

"What is it, Matin?"

"This." She stretched out and put her arms around his neck, kissing him deeply with soft, hungry lips, her breasts flattened against him. "I want you to come with me now, to press me to the earth, to rock me, pillage me."

"That's what I'd like to do too," Shell said, touching the lobe of her ear with the tip of his tongue. Something in his voice got the message across to Matin.

"We cannot?"

"Not tonight. Not right now."

125

"But why?" She drew away, looking up into his face with some confusion.

"There's something I have to do tonight. And it has to do with the safety of your people. I don't think you would want anything to stand in the way of that, would you, Matin?"

"No," she shook her head, "of course not—but what do you mean, Shelter Morgan? Do you mean you are taking the men out to fight tonight?"

"No, not the men. Just me. I want to hit Realto again. I want to confuse and terrorize him."

"And so you will," she said limply.

"And so I will." He kissed her lightly on the forehead, hugged her tightly for one brief moment and turned to walk back to the camp.

There were nine sticks of dynamite left and Shelter sat down not far from the fire to fuse them—with three inches of quick fuse. When he was finished, he stuffed them into his shirt, patted his pocket to make sure he had matches, and rose.

He took his rifle from the saddle scabbard, patted the gray and headed off down the trail. He didn't make it very far. Rounding the first bend he came face to face with Kaska.

"What are you doing now? Running away?"

"Don't be a fool, Kaska."

"I think I am not such a fool as those who believe you, Shelter Morgan, those who trust your magic and your war ability."

"And the others—"

"What others?"

"You know what I'm talking about. I'm talking about

126

Matin. That's what you've got against me, face it."

Kaska uttered a low growl and moved in closer. They were nearly chest to chest on that narrow trail, lighted dimly by the pale rising moon.

"All right," Morgan said at length. "You want your fight. Later then, Kaska, when we're done with this war—then you can have it any way you want. Bare hands, knives, spears. Does that satisfy you?"

"It makes me happy," the Tamaulipa answered. "Happy to know there will come a day when your blood shall flow down this mountain in rivulets."

"Or yours, Kaska. Or yours."

"Yes." He admitted the possibility. "Only do not forget this bargain we have made, Shelter Morgan. I will not, I promise you."

Then he stepped away, letting Shell ease past him on the narrow path. Minutes later when Morgan looked back Kaska was still standing there, bathed in moonlight, watching after him.

Shell shrugged thoughts of Kaska aside—that could be handled when it came up. Maybe. For now he focused on what must be done this night to even up the odds a little.

Realto wouldn't be hard to find, confident in their numbers and superior weaponry they continued to build huge campfires like red beacons against the dark land. Shelter headed toward them, moving silently yet swiftly. There were men in that camp who would not live to see the sun rise, but Morgan felt not a hint of compassion for them. The only soldier he had considered worthy to live had been sent away. Mando was gone, the rest were no better than animals.

He crept up a densely overgrown slope and was sud-

127

denly looking directly into the camp of the invader. He looked hopefully around for Realto or Gato Hernandez, but saw neither of the leaders.

He saw a few men he did know, including Carlos, the man he had exchanged bows with in the mess hall. Shelter scooted back down the slope a few feet and rolled onto his back, pulling three sticks of dynamite from his shirt front. Calmly he extracted a match from his shirt pocket and thumbed it to life.

He touched the flame to the fuse of the first charge and hurled it up and over the bank. He was lighting the second fuse before the first had hit.

Suddenly there was panic in the camp, someone cried out a warning and the first stick blew. Shelter lifted up into a crouch and winged the last stick of dynamite toward the camp as the second charge blew, vomiting flame and thunder. Men ran toward safety, not knowing where safety was, where the attack was coming from. They were cast into strong relief by the gouting yellow flame. A bandit was hurled past Shell's eyes—a leg was missing. His face was white, dead, demonic. Others lay against the earth, trying to scrabble for cover.

The third charge went and they were blown down like nine-pins, hurled against the trees, waves of orange and yellow flame washing over them.

Then there was nothing. The night was black, only the lingering cries marring the silence. The scent of burned flesh and hair, of detonated explosives filled the air.

Shelter was down the slope, circling wide to the east, making toward the second camp, hoping that Realto would be there, that the war could be ended right now. He doubted these already disillusioned, cowardly men would continue on without their leader.

A shot was fired over his head and then dozens of rifles cut loose, but Morgan could tell they were shooting at random, hoping to hold back the beast which prowled the jungle, killing with explosive slashes of its claws.

The night beast. The warrior. Shelter Morgan.

The rifle fire continued unabated as Morgan crawled along a ledge clotted with tangled vines. Just above him was a body of men. The second camp, he thought. He could hear the rapid-fire Spanish with one word recurring over and over. "Realto . . . Realto says . . . screw Realto!"

Shelter looked up and behind him, his back pressed to the bank. He could actually see a sombrero silhouetted against the sky, so near did one of them stand to the edge of the bluff.

"You'd better run, *hombres*," Morgan said, his voice low, conversational as he struck a match and touched it to the fuse.

"What! Who is that?"

"Down there, open fire!" an excited voice urged. Then Shell lobbed the stick of dynamite up and over. The sparkling fuse caught their eyes and they screamed in terror.

"Run! Run, Pablo . . ."

Pablo might have been running, but he didn't get far. The dynamite went off with an earth-shattering explosion, flame washing against the sky as Shelter hugged the bank. Far distant were more cries, of pain, of anger, of command.

Morgan ducked low, headed downslope and angled toward the third fire, knowing that Realto had to be there. There or running in panic through the night-jungle.

He scrambled up onto the level ground and instantly went flat, seeing the men charging in his direction from the still-firelit camp. They had no idea where they were going, but by chance they had stumbled upon their prey. Chance wasn't going to be good enough to take him.

Before his elbows had settled, Morgan had his Winchester up. His first shot pierced the skull of the man on his left, blowing out the back of his skull like an exploding melon. Continuing to rapid fire, Shell switched his sights, levering through and squeezing off two rounds at the second man.

The first missed high, whining off a tree, the second plowed a deadly gulley up his chest and through the throat, unhinging his jaw. Without pausing to sight, Shelter fired once more at the third soldier. He caught it in the groin and went down with a scream of horrible agony. Shell couldn't blame him much for crying out with pain. He placed a mercy round through the soldier's skull and moved on, staying in a crouch, happy for the moment that he hadn't had much time to whip this rabble into a semblance of an army.

As they were they weren't worth much. Guns blasted from all angles—as likely as not they were shooting their own people. Morgan knew damned well he was the only enemy abroad on this night and the bullets that were scything the trees weren't aimed at him, though by chance some came too close for comfort.

He went suddenly flat again. Weaving through the trees as slugs from the Villa force traced red streamers against the night, he came suddenly upon the third

130

camp—and across the clearing, pistol in hand, suspenders down around his knees, dark hair in his eyes, stood Realto, surrounded by a dozen confused, panicked soldiers.

Shell lay pressed against the moon-shadowed earth, scooping the dynamite from his shirt. This was it, the chance to end it before any more Tamaulipas were hurt and he wasn't going to pass up the opportunity.

He lay on his back, listening to the constant crackling of gunfire, lighting the fuse to his first stick. He had his arm cocked back, ready to toss when he heard the anguished voice.

"I do not know. I do not know where he is, what he plans! I know nothing at all, please believe me. Don't!"

There was a scream of pain and Realto's calm voice saying, "Again." Then again came the pain-ridden scream and Shelter pinched off the fuse. They had Mando.

Wriggling forward a little he could see the kid on the ground, a dark worm of blood running from the corner of his mouth, his eyes wide and frightened. The soldier standing over him kicked Mando again and the cry of pain again echoed chillingly through the night.

Shelter lay there cursing through his teeth. The damned idiot had come back, after all Shell had told him, he still came back. Back to be a soldier, a man, one of the people's revolutionaries. And now they were kicking his teeth out for him.

He had balled up the whole attack. Now the only sensible thing to do was to pull out silently and make his way back to the Tamaulipa village.

Sensible, if you didn't hold a man's life to be worth

131

anything. Shelter Morgan did. He had to get the kid out of there, tear him away from Villa's people one more time, hoping that now he had learned his lesson.

Shell backed away fifty feet or so. There, in a crouch, he lit the fuse to a stick of dynamite and lobbed it far to the east. Moving in a half circle, he paused, lit another and winged it off into the jungle.

The shots around him multiplied rapidly. Thousands of rounds were being fired off in all directions. Confusion was rampant, which was exactly Shelter's intention. He could see groups of men pounding through the brush and trees, running away from or after something which existed only in their panic-ridden imaginations.

"I told you they weren't disciplined, Villa."

Morgan crept through the trees, coming up on the far side of the clearing where he had seen Realto. The general was gone now. A single guard stood next to the prone Mando Sandoval, holding his rifle loosely, barrel downward, looking off into the trees.

With all the shooting going on, Morgan's own shot wasn't even heard. It sure wasn't heard by the guard who was slammed to the earth as the .44-40 ripped through his heart and lungs.

With his eyes flashing around the perimeter, finger on the trigger of the Winchester, Morgan moved into the clearing. He didn't waste time on gentleness. If Mando survived what they had already done to him, he would survive a little rough handling.

Morgan grabbed his collar and began dragging him the hell out of there. He wasn't qute fast enough. Four soldiers burst into the clearing opposite him and Shell touched off, gutting one man as the others fell back, firing wildly.

Shell yanked Mando after him into the shelter of the trees, paused to empty the magazine of his rifle in the direction of the pursuit and started on again. There was one stick of dynamite left and he let them have it for good luck, covering his retreat as he shouldered Mando and started back at a killing jog-trot for the Tamualipa village high above.

12.

They came with the dawn. Standing on the wind-swept ledge with Kaska and Itza beside him Shelter could see the long, wavering line of approaching soldiers.

"You did not frighten them so much last night," Kaska said mockingly.

"Oh they're scared enough," Morgan responded. "But they're more scared of going back and reporting to Villa what a failure this has been."

"How is the boy?" Itza asked.

"He's all right. A few broken ribs, a bad crease on his skull, but he's all right. Matin is seeing to him. I don't think," Morgan added, "that he'll have much of an itch to be a soldier after this."

"What does it matter how this boy feels," Kaska said sourly. "What of the battle? Are we prepared?"

"I hope so. Itza, do the men at the dynamite caches know what to do?"

"Yes, Shelter Morgan."

"You're sure?"

"I am sure."

"Then we're all right. We've got the edge and Realto, if he's got any sense at all, should know it."

"Still they will come," Itza said.

"Yes. Still they will come. Let's get ready to meet them

when they do."

Morgan wasn't prepared yet to settle in behind the gatling gun. It was the last resort, the Tamaulipa redoubt. He hoped that Realto would back off, seeing that this was one hell of a position to assault. As little sympathy as he had for the Villa soldiers who would die, he had no liking for the slaughter which was sure to come of this. Somewhere they had mothers, brothers, wives, children who might even care about them, bastards that they were.

Shell, with Itza, began to climb toward the highlands. From there they could see the winding trail, the brown-clad soldiers working their way uphill, the sunlight glinting on rifle barrels, belt buckles, brass buttons.

"They will never stop," Itza said. "Sometimes I think our way of life is ending. If not these men then another army will come. They will not leave us alone. They wish all people to live the same, to think the same, and so they will come."

Shelter didn't say anything. Silently he agreed with the Tamaulipas. One day the Mexican army might come. Governments find it easier to rule when all people are locked into the same set of rules, their way of life regulated, uniform.

Shelter got down on his belly, Itza doing the same. Their eyes followed the soldiers who tramped upward, following the path along the side of the volcano.

Shell, looking back across his shoulder could see the warrior crouched down by the first dynamite charge. It would take that to slow them down, he thought. That and more.

The sweat ran down Shelter's throat, trickled across his eyebrows as they lay pressed against the stone. Below them now were the soldiers of Hector Villa. Below them and still marching. The last man was past before Itza touched Shell's shoulder and he glanced back to see the Tamaulipa who had been watching the dynamite sprint up over the ridge.

"He's lit it, let's go," Shell said.

They moved out themselves, heading for the high, serrated ridge. Achieving it they stood watching. Nothing at all happened for an incredible length of time. Seconds became hours. Through a gap in the rocks Shelter could see the men in sweat-stained uniforms marching silently uphill.

Then the charge went and he could see nothing. Nothing but dust, flying rocks. The shock waves from the detonation, warm, shuddering, passed over Shell, tugging at his shirt. It was like a blast of desert wind. Up there.

Below it was like the assault of hell. Rocks flew through the air, smashing bone and skull. Men were crushed by the triggered landslide, swept off the side of the mountain to cartwheel through space, seeing the death below them, their throats constricted, shutting off their death screams.

"Come on," Morgan said, and his face was as grim as Itza's. They had come looking for death, but still it was horrible to watch.

It slowed Realto, but didn't stop him. Two-thirds of his men had made it through and now they began firing their guns as they moved up, chasing away the spectres of death, perhaps—there were no Indians in sight.

The second charge went off before Shell had settled in behind the gatling gun. This one was larger, and it sent spumes of rock dust and earth clouding into the skies; from where Shelter sat waiting to deliver still more death

136

to the invaders, he could see half a dozen men—or parts of them—blown off into the chasm at their feet, see the massive landslide slough off tons of rock which slid down and blocked the trail.

Still Realto came on—what madness had overtaken him? The need to kill, to strike back, to hurt the other as the other had hurt him.

They came on blindly, charging up the trail. Shelter looked up, seeing his Indians on the rocks above the trail, their bows and arrows, spears, blowguns ready.

Shelter saw the first men round the bend, saw the face of Gato Hernandez, sweat-streaked, whiskered, wild. Beside him was Realto on his black horse. They were within a hundred yards and Morgan let them come. From the rocks above the poison darts started to rain down and soldiers fell writhing to the ground to be trampled on by those behind them. They charged on blindly, knowing that there was no retreat possible any longer. It was victory or death and so they came on.

Fifty yards. Shelter blew the dust off the bottom of the magazine, snapped it into the breech and snuggled down.

They were within a hundred feet of him when he cranked the handle down and the murderous fire of the gatling sprayed the trail with death and destruction. They hadn't known about the gatling, couldn't have, and it was with shock and horror that they realized they were getting just what they had planned for the Tamaulipas.

The magazine emptied, Shell yanked it out and reloaded smoothly. The barrels of the gatling spat flame and violent death, shredding the soldiers who rushed his position.

Yes, it was training, all right. Of a sort. He had been told to show these bastards how to use a gatling, and now

137

they were learning. Too late. A line of crimson stitches appeared across the chest of Realto's black horse and the animal went down, killing a foot soldier with its slashing hoofs. Realto lay unmoving on the ground.

Shell fired and reloaded, picking up a fresh magazine from the neat stack he had at his right hand. He fired, the bellowing of the big gun deafening, the smoke burning his eyes, the screams of the dead and dying in his ears.

There were a dozen or so men left when he stopped cranking. They stood there almost impassively—the remainder of Villa's army of liberation—waiting to die, and it was beyond Morgan to do them.

"Cease fire!" he shouted in a cracked voice. "Hold it! You, throw down your weapons!"

They did so with alacrity and relief, and stood there dazed, stupefied by the carnage around them. Gunsmoke and rock dust still floated through the air.

A hair-raising howl filled the air and Kaska, spear in hand appeared, leaping toward the prisoners. "Kill them!" he howled, "slice them to dog meat. Burn them."

"No!" Shelter rose from behind the gun, his face blackened with powder smoke, his mouth compressed, eyes hard. "We have won the battle. We don't need to slaughter helpless men to prove that we are stronger."

"I have said that we will kill them." Kaska demonstrated his point. He stepped forward and ran his spear through the gut of a soldier who had been standing, trembling, hands raised.

Shelter uttered a low growl and hurled himself at Kaska. He had wanted his fight—all right, damnit, the time had come.

Kaska tried to wrench his spear free, but the head wouldn't come. He snapped the shaft off and swung at

138

Morgan's face with the jagged end of it. Shell felt the splintered tip of it rake his cheek as he side-stepped and kicked out with a booted foot which caught Kaska on the knee.

The Tamaulipa cried out with rage and pain. He drew a long, thin-bladed knife from behind his belt and slashed out at Morgan.

Behind him Shelter heard an uproar, heard Itza shouting: "No! Let them fight."

Shell's hands dropped to his belt knife. The bowie glinted in the sunlight as he unsheathed. Kaska's eyes narrowed with caution as the two men circled each other warily.

Below was a drop of nearly two thousand feet, above the rising cliff face. There was nowhere to run. And neither man wanted it that way. The prisoners stood staring at the two adversaries. Behind them the Tamaulipas watched.

Kaska lunged and Shell parried the blow, their knives ringing as they met. Shell kicked out at Kaska's groin, but the Indian twisted away from the attempt. Kaska was crouched low, his knife point flicking out like a snake's tongue as he probed for an opening.

Shell didn't mean to give him one. He made a feint toward Kaska's belly and then slashed up viciously with the razor-edged bowie. A thin scarlet line appeared on Kaska's chin and the Indian wiped at it angrily as Shell slashed down hard, trying to sever Kaska's knife hand.

Kaska leaped back quickly, but Shelter followed up, jumping in, the bowie overhead. He caught Kaska's wrist and held the deadly blade of the Tamaulipa's knife away from his body while Kaska's fumbling fingers gripped Shell's knife, a knife which was slowly descending toward

Kaska's terrified face.

They stood chest to chest, muscles knotted, tendons standing taut, hearts pumping wildly. Kaska strained to keep the descending knife away, but Shell's strength was too much for him.

The blade approached inexorably. Kaska's eyes were wide, filled with hatred. The point of the knife blade touched the bronzed, veined skin of the Indian's throat, and maybe at that moment he thought of their first meeting when Kaska had been so eager to drive his spear through Morgan's throat. Maybe he remembered and cursed those who had stopped him as with a last effort, Morgan drove the bowie in and Kaska's blood gushed out.

Shell yanked the knife free and stepped back panting. Kaska nodded at him, dropped his own knife to clatter against the stone and then toppled over, spinning through the chasm at his feet to land a thousand feet below against the black, unyielding stone and lie there dead.

Morgan backed away from the edge, turning slowly to see what sorts of ideas the rest of the Tamaulipas might have. They had treated him fairly up to this point—but then he had never killed one of them before.

The warriors stood in a tense ring staring at Morgan. From the village Matin came running, her breasts swaying and bobbing. It was Itza who broke the tenseness.

"They fought together. It was a good fight. Shelter Morgan won fairly. Now we must work. Clean the rocks off the trail. We will do what we can while the daylight holds. Now," he said sharply, "do what can be done!"

He came to where Morgan stood. "You, what will you do now? Will you live with us and take Matin for your

140

woman? Will you become our war leader?"

"No. No, Itza. If the tribe is fortunate, you will be made war chief yourself. I still have other battles."

"These men from North America."

"Yes."

Itza nodded with understanding. He looked at the prisoners. "What should be done with these?"

"It's up to you, I suppose. What I would tell you to do is take their weapons and let them go. They have been lucky, and they know it. I do not think they will return to the land of the Tamaulipas."

"Let them go?" Itza shrugged and smiled. That was a new thought to him, apparently. "As you say, it will be done. I think," he added softly, "first we shall keep them in the stockade for a time. I will show them the heads of my old enemies and let them worry a little longer for their skins."

Before Shell could answer Matin was to him, her arms around his neck, her head buried in the hollow of his shoulder. "You are all right?"

"I'm fine," he assured her.

"You are bleeding."

Shell hadn't even noticed it. Kaska had tagged him with the knife. Across his forearm was a deep, narrow furrow. Blood trickled down between his knuckles.

"We must clean that up."

"All right." They walked together toward the village. The women and children were returning from the hills now and the place seemed to take on life, to be renewed.

"You are leaving soon," Matin said.

"Yes."

"I see this in your eyes. I know it, as I knew you would leave. But you will be back. I see that too."

"Sure," he said, only half-believing it.

"There is time before you leave," she said, halting to stand before him and look up intently. "There is time for you to make one last pledge to Matin."

"There is time," Shelter answered with a smile.

There was time for them to climb the hill to the warrior's hut once again, for Shelter Morgan to lay her down, to go down beside her, for Matin to throw a lazy leg high into the air, giving him access to her body as he eased forward and in, time for her body to heat and writhe, to clutch at his demandingly, to drain him and ask for more.

And then there was no more time. It was time for the war to go on, for the blood-letting to begin anew. The happy spirits drifted away on tiny wings and the dark, brooding, killing things hovered over Shelter and Matin.

He stopped to visit Mando who was sitting up, tended to by a slender woman of thirty who explained, "I have lost my son, I have lost my father, I have lost my husband, it is good for me to have someone to care for."

Mando watched Shelter enter and hunker down beside him. His eyes were sunken, unhappy, uncertain.

"Well, how you feeling, kid?" Shell asked, looking at the gash which split open Mando's scalp and ran across most of his forehead. His cheek was bruised—it was a wonder it wasn't crushed. Realto's boot had landed with some force.

"I am well enough," he said. His tone of voice was dark and gloomy. Someone might have told him he was dying the way he talked.

"Mando, you're lucky. You're young and healthy. You've taken some abuse and come through it. You've been disillusioned, but you've only started living, kid."

142

"No. My life is over. What do I do? Go home and tell everyone I was a fool."

"Not a fool. A man who made a mistake. Show me one who hasn't."

"The old people . . ."

"The old people have made mistakes. They'll be a lot more understanding than you seem to believe. If they're not, then they're not worth worrying about. You seem to have the idea that since this was a bust you have to go back to being what you were before—an unhappy kid in a small pueblo. You don't. You can go most anywhere you please, do what you want. Just don't pin your hopes on any tin gods, Mando. Walk your own road."

"And you?"

"I walk my own road, kid. It's a dark and winding road, but I walk it. Maybe just because I started down it one day and it's a long way back."

"I'm asking about Villa. Villa and the Willits brothers."

"I know you are, Mando. They're at the end of that road waiting for me."

"I don't understand you. Why keep on fighting?"

"He's still got a good-sized force back there, Mando. Enough to make someone trouble, enough to go on killing. And there'll be new recruits coming in. Men . . ."

"Men like me."

"Yes. Some of them. Others who are just plain hard and as evil as Villa. I can't allow it, kid. I won't."

"And the woman," Mando said quietly.

"Yes, there's Bonita Madrid. I think of her living with that pig, the man who killed her family, smashed her world, moved right in to her house and took her for his mistress—I think of her sitting in her room at night, her

143

heart in her throat, knowing that he's out there, that maybe tonight he'll come."

"I would like to go with you," Mando said.

"No."

"I can fight!"

"You couldn't stamp a cockroach to death right now, Mando," Shelter answered.

"In a few days . . ."

"I don't think Bonita has a few more days. She's tough, but how much can anyone take? No, it won't do to wait, Mando. I doubt we got every single member of this expedition. That's not the way things work out. Somewhere there'll be a man or two, a dozen of them who said to hell with it and hid out. They'll be on their way back to tell Villa what happened. Lying to convince him of their own bravery. He'll know, Mando. And with Villa it will be enough to trigger off a madness, a rage. There'll be a bloodbath because of this. That's the way Villa thinks. When he's hurt he strikes back. Somewhere there are other people in his way, and they'll pay the price."

"Unless you stop him."

"Do you see anyone else trying?" Shell exhaled sharply. Resting his hand on Mando's he said. "Get well, kid. Get well and go out and find yourself the kind of world you want to live in. It's there somewhere."

Morgan rose and started toward the door. Outside it was nearly dark, a few stars blinking on against the cobalt blue sky. He had already ducked to clear the lintel when Mando spoke.

"Thank you." There was a catch in his voice. Shelter didn't look back, but simply nodded and went out into the night to stand looking around the Tamaulipa village. There were three big bonfires burning, and men danced

144

around them as others were served food and drink by the women. There was the chatter of happy voices, relieved voices speaking all at once. The tribe had survived. They celebrated their life and praised their gods. Shell wondered how long they could continue to survive with the new world bearing down on them.

He saw Matin across the clearing, sitting beside her father, arms looped around her knees. She seemed to see him, to pick him out of the darkness. Shelter turned his back and walked away. It was time to make war, not love.

13.

The house was still there. It was incredible. It seemed to be left over from another time. A lot had happened in the past few days. Shelter sat his horse on the beach north of the Madrid house. Or was it the Villa house? No, he could live in it, but he couldn't ever own it, not like the man who'd earned it, seen to the planting of the gardens, the careful placement of the tiles. Villa was a destroyer. Destroyers don't own anything in this world.

Morgan looked at the house, saw the lights burning not much brighter than the distant stars. He looked the promontory over carefully. He hadn't tried it from this side, from the north, but only from the south, out of Escebar. Now that trail was closed to him. There was no chance of bluffing his way past the guards this time. They would be fully alerted, have their orders to kill.

He doubted the horse could make it up from this side, and as he drew nearer, he became certain. He wasn't all that sure a man afoot could make that climb.

The promontory rose steeply, all weather-pocked sandstone, covered with jungle the first half of the way. After that it was open ground, nearly straight up. And there would be guards prowling, had to be.

Shelter rode the gray inland, picketed it in a dense thicket, unsaddled and slipped the bit.

146

He patted the horse's flank, wondering if he would ever see it again. Then, placing his hat beside his saddle he moved out, silent and swift in the darkness, moving across the shadowed beach as the moon screamed out warnings.

He was at the base of the promontory fifteen minutes later, crouched down, panting, clinging to the shadows there. He looked up, seeing the tangle of growth, the bare, sheer rock above. The house was out of view. He waited there for half an hour, eyes straining against the night, watching for guards along the bluff, seeing none.

Of course if they were any good you wouldn't see them. Not until you poked your head over the top and they opened up, blowing you off the bluff.

Gritting his teeth, Shelter started up, shaking with a chill which wasn't of the weather. The night was warm, balmy, a mild breeze off the sea shifting the leaves of the trees around him.

The chill didn't last long—it never did—and Shell began to climb methodically, using the vines, the trees to aid him. He slithered upslope, the sweat raining off of him. He stopped abruptly—had he heard something?

He waited, watching, but it must have been only the night-boogers stirring. Little fear-born mischief makers. He was bathed in sweat by the time he reached the naked bluff above the trees. He eyed it carefully, searching for the best way up.

It was all pocked by wind and rain. Footholds and handholds everywhere. But it was sheer and dangerous. To be discovered up there, clinging to naked rock would mean death. They could merrily pot away until they had shot the life out of him and his nerveless fingers lost their grip on the stone and he fell away to the beach far,

far below.

He moved out, his stomach tightening, his eyes lifting constantly to the dark rim above. He nearly lost his grip once. The sandstone, soft enough to be honeycombed as it was, was soft enough to crumble away in his hands.

Yet in another ten minutes he was up. He lifted his head over the rim, looked quickly right and left and rolled up, drawing his Colt as he lay on his back in the darkness, his heart hammering in his ears.

Nothing.

There was no sound, no shadow of movement and Morgan scraped himself up and made a dash for the trees beyond. There again he paused, his every sense alert for threat. Nothing—Morgan frowned. Could even Villa's sloppy army be this sloppy? Content that the bluff was steep, that no attacking force could effectively scale it.

They should have been alert for a single man. They should have known Shelter Morgan would be back.

Or maybe not! It took a while to soak in, but Shell realized that Villa *wouldn't* think that way. Why would a lone man attempt to storm his fortress? Maybe Jim Pike was not what he had pretended to be, but Villa wouldn't believe a man alone would attack his stronghold. As for Willits, the odds were very good that he hadn't yet connected Jim Pike with Shelter Morgan.

If he had he would have known—known that Morgan would be back. And back again until Zack Willits was buried and a-mouldering in his grave.

Shell was near the greenhouse, but in the trees where the shadows cut the moonlight which seemed beacon-bright atop the promontory.

He could hear music from the house. The faltering chords of a piano being picked at. Bonita. She was there still, kept like an animal, a pet for the blood-thirsty one.

He thought of going that way, of finishing it now, but even a casual inspection revealed a man on the roof, one walking his rounds near the house, one sitting on an upstairs balcony, hat tugged low, rifle cradled in his arms.

Not just yet, he thought.

He came out of the trees behind the little cottage which had been his not many days earlier. The barracks beyond were ablaze with light. Shell heard a guitar pounding away, hoots of laughter. Villa had replenished his force, it seemed, and the new batch was no better than the old.

Which suited Morgan perfectly. He moved through the shadows toward the dynamite shed. There was a guard standing watch there, but he was very bored, very inattentive. He didn't even react as the shadowy figure separated itself from the surrounding darkness, slipped up behind him and neatly sliced his throat with a bowie which had done that particular job more than once.

Shell dragged the body around to the back of the shed, lifted the guard's rifle and returned to the door. With his knife he pried the hasp off the door and swung it open, slipping inside by moonlight.

It was musty, low-roofed, empty—but for the three cases of explosives stacked neatly in one corner.

Morgan hefted one and slipped out, moving back toward the bluffs beyond the greenhouse. He hid it in a cleft near where he had made his climb and stood breathing deeply, looking toward the big house. It had to be done, and it had to be done now before someone stumbled across that body.

Bonita Madrid had proven her courage. She had done a job for the Mexican government as well as Shelter's own, reporting Villa's schemes, counting heads and guns. Now, however, she was coming out of there, like it or not.

He started toward the house once more, pausing frequently to search the darkness ahead of him. There were several soldiers roaming the garden. Inside the house Villa would be relaxing after dinner, perhaps with the Willits brothers as his guests.

Or maybe they weren't relaxing. Perhaps word had reached them of the jungle war—though Shell was hoping that wasn't the case, hoping on horseback he had beaten any returning stragglers.

He didn't like this set-up, didn't like it one bit. Penetration would be difficult, escape hazardous to the extreme. He liked the idea of that young lady being held in that house less.

Shell moved; crossing a small grassy area he entered the cedar trees opposite. He pulled up there, drawing his Colt. One of the guards was walking nearer, backlighted by the illuminated window on this side of the house.

Shell pulled back behind the tree, pistol held beside his ear. When the guard walked by, Morgan brought that gun down hard.

It rang off the guard's skull and he slumped to the earth, Shelter catching him by the shoulders before he had hit the ground, dragging him into the trees. There he appropriated the Mexican's sombrero and his rifle.

Then casually he began walking the guard's round. He studied the house on all sides as he moved. The ground floor windows were iron-barred, so he would have to go up—unless he wanted to take the chance of kicking in Villa's front door and walking on through.

Somehow the notion didn't appeal to him.

"Jose?"

The voice caused Shelter's muscles to tighten. He hadn't even seen the soldier. He was leaning casually against an adobe out-building, a bottle in his hand. He gestured with his fingers and Shelter started that way.

"Want a drink . . . ?" Shelter's rifle butt cracked the Mexican's teeth out for him and his head thudded back against the adobe wall. He slid slowly down and Shelter towed him to the back of the building, thinking that he was leaving quite a trail now—how long would it be before someone discovered that one of the three men was missing?

If Villa caught him, the thoughts Kaska had had about how to treat a prisoner would look like a child's. Villa had the madness it takes to be truly cruel, to take perverted pleasure in another human being's pain.

Morgan had to decide quickly, and he thought he knew now what he would do. There was a rose trellis at the southeast corner, and it might have been made for climbing, so accessible was it. If the wood wasn't rotten . . . Shelter reached the corner, slung the rifle over his shoulder, let the sombrero hang down his back on its drawstring, and started up, seeing the balcony above, the dark french window beyond.

He stepped over the balustrade, glancing back at the moonlit yard below. Going to the french window he tried the latch and found it locked. He slipped his knife from its sheath and jammed it in the space between door and frame—and immediately drew back. Someone was in the room.

Now a light went on and he heard another voice. Getting down low where a casual glance was least likely to pick him up, Shelter peered into the room through the scarlet, floor-length draperies.

He tensed as he saw the broad back, recognized the language as English. Zack Willits and one of his brothers, and in Shell's hand was his Colt.

And he couldn't do a damned thing about it. To take Zack out he would have to make noise, alert the house, lose the chance of getting Bonita out of there.

"Screw that Mexican," Zack Willits was saying. "Once we hit that army post, we'll be loaded with gold."

The other man muttered something. "You and Ben both, the pair of you, you worry too much," Zack Willits said scornfully.

"Yeah, well where in hell is Hardy then?"

"Don't worry about Hardy. I guess he can take care of himself." Zack turned toward the window, and for a minute Shell thought those dark, evil eyes had seen him beneath the curtains. Logic told him it was impossible. It was light in the room, dark on the balcony, only Shell's eye could have been seen beneath the drapes—logic said it was impossible, but still Morgan's heart jumped and his hand tightened involuntarily on the butt of that Colt.

He backed away and straightened up, looking above him to the roof. The trellis ran that far, but there was a guard up there. Morgan had seen him earlier. A guard above and now one below. Shelter heard the hiss then. Crouching down in the darkness, he saw the Mexican prowling around below, probably looking for the missing man and his bottle of mescal.

Shell let him wander away and then he decided—up it would be.

Shoving the Colt away he clambered up the trellis. The guard saw him almost as soon as he reached the roof. The rifle came around sharply.

"Who is it?"

"Jose," Shell murmured, shuffling toward him.

"What the hell are you doing up here?" The guard drew himself up, ready to deliver a lecture to Jose. Jose didn't listen. He drew his bowie knife and drove it into the guard's heart. The guard fell. Shelter, tangled up in his legs, followed. The guard's rifle slid down the red-tiled roof and dropped over the side, eluding Shelter's scrabbling fingers.

He cursed slowly, deeply. A missing man might not be noticed for a while—not with this bunch—there were lots of reasons for a man being away from his post. With a rifle lying on the ground it was a different story. Not even this kind of soldier walked off and left his rifle.

And there would be blood on that one.

It was all over Shell as he moved in a crouch across the roof until he came to a second balcony. He bent low and peered over the eaves. No lights, and listening, no sound. Was that Bonita's room? He just didn't know.

Taking the chance he turned, and gripping the edge of the roof, dropped off briefly into space before landing with a muffled thud on the balcony. He stayed there a moment, eyes cutting the darkness, but he had not been seen.

He applied the bowie to the latch and slipped into the room. With relief he smelled the lilac, the jasmine, the scents of a woman. He moved toward the bed, touched it and found it empty, covered with a satin spread. He waited as his eyes adjusted to the darkness, listening to the vague, distorted sounds from downstairs.

It was Bonita's room he now saw—there was no doubt of it. A lovely sheer white nightgown lay on the foot of the bed, a pair of white slippers on the floor beneath it.

Then all that was necessary was to sit and wait for

her—but damnit, how much time could he have? How long would Villa keep her downstairs, listening to his mad rambling?

Shelter took a chance. Crossing to the door he turned the heavy bronze knob and opened it a crack. He saw the red carpet on the landing, and below the fireplace, Villa seated, lifting a glass of wine in a drunken toast. Villa's back was to him, Bonita was to his left, three quarters away from Shell.

There were six or seven others down there. Two in uniform, the rest in civilian clothing. Shelter recognized the mayor of Escebar among them.

Too many to try it—he had thought that a drunken Villa might be taken unaware, clubbed down and disposed of. But that just wouldn't play.

Then by chance, or by some subtle awareness Bonita's head slowly turned. She looked directly at the door to her room and Shelter chanced it. He opened the door a good foot, showing himself plainly before closing it again.

It was up to her now. There was nothing else he could do. He promised himself that he would give her five minutes and if she wasn't there by then he would pull out.

She was there in two.

She was across the room in less than that, clinging to Shell, soft and warm, jasmine scented, her breasts rising and falling with undefined emotion.

"Get out of those clothes."

"What?"

"Get into something you can ride in. We're getting the hell out of here."

"But I . . ."

"You've done enough. What do you want to do, wait

154

around until he hurts you during one of his fits?"

"He's getting worse," she admitted, glancing back toward the door.

"Move it. We don't have much time."

"All right," she said deciding quickly. Downstairs something crashed against the floor. Shell heard a moan and then a shout.

"Hurry up."

She was already out of her dress, and now Bonita yanked a divided riding skirt and a white blouse out of the closet. "Haven't you got anything darker."

"Oh." She looked at the white blouse, nodded her understanding and got on something that would make less of a target out there.

Bonita crossed the room, yanking the pins from her hair, digging a pair of boots out from under the bed. The sound of footsteps on the staircase jerked her head up. She looked with anguish at Shelter who crossed to the door and locked it.

In a moment the knob rattled, there was a muffled curse and then the shout.

"What are you doing that takes so long?" Hector Villa's voice demanded from the other side of the door. The knob was rattled again.

"I'll be right there," Bonita promised.

"The light's out. Why have you got the light out? And the door locked!"

There was another thump and for a minute Shelter thought the revolutionary leader was going to force the door and come on through. It would end the revolution right quick if he did—unfortunately it would also very probably be the end of Shelter Morgan.

"Please," Bonita said. "Just woman business, I'll be

155

right down. A very few minutes."

"See that you are. What good are you if you can't even stay by me? What good are you anyway? I wonder that. Can you hear me?" The fist pounded twice on the door.

"Yes, yes, I hear you. You are right." Bonita stamped her feet into her boots as she spoke. Morgan held his thumb over the hammer of his big blue Colt, not knowing—you never know what a man like Villa will do.

Finally, drunkenly, he said, "Get down here. One minute or you will get the same as last night—only worse, Bonita, I promise you that!"

Then, with a final thump on the door he walked away. Shell remained where he was, listening to the receding footsteps. Then, satisfied, he crossed the room.

"What happened last night?" he asked, taking Bonita by the shoulders, but she looked down, shaking her head without answering.

"Okay. Let's get the hell out of here. And fast."

Villa had just speeded up Morgan's schedule. Two minutes. Two minutes and he would be back. That gave them approximately two and a half minutes to cross the promontory through the guards and get down the bluff.

"Shelter, can we . . . ?"

Morgan didn't even answer. He took her roughly by the arm and aimed her toward the balcony. Two minutes. Two minutes and the guns would speak again.

Except they didn't get those two minutes. There was a pounding on the door and then the near report of a handgun as Hector Villa blew the lock away.

14.

Shell spun Bonita toward the balcony behind them, "Jump," he told her. There wasn't time to do it cautiously. He saw her eyes, wide with fear, saw the determined nod. Then she was gone, over the balustrade, Shelter standing on the balcony still, Colt in hand.

The door burst open and Shell cut loose, three .44s delivering death. But Villa didn't catch the lead. His head was there, framed in the doorway and then withdrawn as three soldiers piled through, Villa screaming exhortations.

They didn't get the job done. They went down in a tangle, and Shell, giving them one parting shot to remember him by was across the balcony in two strides, over the rail, dropping two stories to land in the dead shrubbery beneath the window.

"Are you . . . ?" Bonita touched his arm and Shelter snarled at her.

"Get moving. North, through the trees."

She left at a run, achieving the cedars as the soldiers rounded the corner of the house noisily. By then Morgan had his rifle unlimbered and he let them have half a dozen rounds. The muzzle of the Winchester spat red flame. A man screamed in pain, a ricochet whined off the wall of the house. Answering shots cut the shrubbery around

Morgan, but they weren't well-aimed. It takes discipline or madness to stand up and exchange shots with the enemy at close range. Shelter Morgan was more disciplined—or madder. He had seen fire fights, seen the death winging his way too many times to count. He had been a soldier of one kind or another for a decade, and this was nothing new—stomach-knotting, pulse-raising, yes, but not new and totally terrifying as it was to Villa's green recruits.

They trampled each other trying to reach the safety of the corner of the house and as they withdrew, Shell backed away toward the cedars, levering six more shots through. Then the rifle clicked down on an empty chamber and Shell dropped it, sliding his Colt free of its holster. He pushed one round through it and then was into the trees, limping toward the bluff. He had jolted his right leg when he landed and now it was giving him trouble.

Voices shouted all around him, an occasional searching shot probed the cedars, whining off the bark of the trees. Somewhere a mad voice roared with rage.

"God, Shelter, I thought . . ."

Bonita was there, her hair hanging loose, her hands held up in a gesture of anguish.

"Keep moving." He turned her bodily and they plodded toward the bluff, Shelter making hard work of it as his leg stabbed with pain.

The soldier was directly in front of them, looming out of the darkness. Shell's muzzle flash illuminated his hard, dark face and the sudden rush of blood from his lips as the .44 bullet tagged meat and bone lower down. The soldier was blown back and Bonita screamed uncontrollably.

"Just a minute." Shelter held her up. "I've left something that I need."

"Shell, for God's sake!"

"You start down."

"I won't leave you."

"Start down, damn it, Bonita. My horse is in the trees a quarter of a mile north. If I'm not there in ten minutes, you take him and head out. Ride until he drops. They'll not catch you on that horse."

"Shell . . ."

"Get!" He gathered her in his arm and kissed her once, finding her mouth warm and moist.

She started down obediently, after one puzzled, searching look. He watched her slide off into the darkness then turned and hobbled to the cleft where he had put the dynamite. It was going to be a bitch getting it down, but he needed it. He ripped the crate open and began stuffing sticks of dynamite into his shirt once again, eyes lifted to the trees where the approaching soldiers were. A roll of fuse he shoved into a hip pocket. He smiled grimly, thinking how he would go if a bullet tagged him. A flash of glorious flame, the peal of explosive thunder, it would be showy at the least. Maybe it was a good way to go. All at once . . .

He roughly forced that thought aside. He wasn't planning on dying, but on living to finish this job, living, perhaps to know Bonita Madrid better, much better.

A soldier burst from the woods and shouted out anxiously: "I've got him!"

And then he got it, all right. Shell palmed his Colt and fired twice. The soldier jerked back like a marionette yanked from the stage.

Shelter got to his feet, and reloading as he ran, made

for the bluff. The moon was glaring on him now, and if he could have he would have shot it out. It was a hunter's moon, and Morgan was the quarry, crippled and alone.

He eased over the edge of the bluff, feeling a stick of dynamite fall from his shirt and roll downslope. Above the voices continued to shout, rising above them the mad cries of Hector Villa.

The Colt had to be holstered. There was no hope of fighting them off now, the only chance was escape. As soon as they discovered he was on the bluff, they had him. The moon was a yellow accusing eye.

Shell went down swiftly, once losing his grip and sliding for thirty feet before he managed to get the brakes on. If he could make the jungle below—the jungle which grew halfway up the bluff and no farther. Shell glanced down—it seemed miles away. He could not see Bonita and that cheered him. She had to be into the trees, safe.

The sky above him was weirdly lighted and it was a second before Morgan realized it was torchlight. They were still searching the trees, apparently.

And then suddenly they were not. A voice cried out with exultation and a bullet sang off the bluff within a foot of Shell's head, spattering him with rock dust. He didn't even bother to look up. Downward. The jungle. That was all that mattered.

A barrage of shots sounded in the night and Shell simultaneously lost his grip. He was slipping, sliding, rolling. He clawed out for a grip of some sort, anything to slow his terrifying descent, but there was nothing. He felt the ground fall away, heard the bark of the rifles and then the sudden roaring in his ears, the flash of flame behind his eyes before the total darkness.

He floated through a black, starlit sea, seeing bits of himself floating here and there. A hand, a blue eye, an unshaven jawbone detached from the rest of his face. And the mouth—the laughing, mocking mouth.

The mouth, he suddenly realized, belonged to Villa and it laughed until the blood spilled out of it and Villa turned into a yellow-striped fish, swimming swiftly away.

The hands reached down from out of the sky, white, tender hands and slowly began putting the parts back together, reassembling what had been Shelter Morgan.

"Shell?"

His eyes blinked open and he saw her face, saw the worry there. Bonita was backlighted by the moon which cast an angelic aura around her head. She was an angel just then. Soft, caring, beautiful.

"Where am I?" Shell sat up.

"Don't try to rise."

He heard a soft whickering sound and turned his head to see his gray standing there. The odd thing was that it had two heads, and a lot of legs—a whole bundle of legs. Shell blinked and shook his head.

"I guess I took quite a rap. What happened?"

"You fell off the bluff. I saw you lose your grip and tumble down the slope. It was terrible. It seemed like there were a hundred guns shooting at you. You know, if you hadn't fallen, I almost think they would have killed you. Funny isn't it?"

"Not too right now," Shell mumbled, trying to stand. A numbing pain shot through his side as he got to his feet with Bonita's help.

"You crashed into the trees and knocked yourself unconscious. I got you down and dragged you up the

161

beach. I thought they would come down the bluff, but it scared them."

"I had any sense it would have scared me too. Come on now," he said, "let's get moving."

"But we're safe here. You can't ride."

"Oh, I can ride. If it's ride or be killed. We're not safe here, Bonita, not safe at all. They didn't want to try the bluff, but they'll be on their way around the promontory by now, you can bet on it."

He began unloading his shirt, placing the dynamite into his saddlebags and Bonita let out a sort of gurgling noise. "I knew you had something . . . but not that."

"It's gotten to be a habit lately," Shell cracked. "I seem to be carrying the stuff everywhere I go."

"You could have . . . you could have . . ."

"Yeah, I could have." Shell stepped into the saddle stiffly, his leg and side protesting vigorously. "Come on—" he offered Bonita a helping hand.

"We should wait. You should rest a while, Shelter."

"Do you think so?" He was smiling, his eyes lifted toward the beach beyond the trees. Bonita, looking that way saw the long dark line of horsemen rounding the promontory. She took Shell's hand and swung up behind as Morgan urged the gray forward, taking it deeper into the dark, concealing jungle.

An hour later they were on a high knoll where they had a commanding view of the country below them. Nothing was stirring near them. Villa's men were staying near the beach, almost as if they didn't want to find Morgan— maybe they didn't.

Shell stood watching the land for a while by moonlight and then eased down onto the ground, hurting everyplace it's possible to hurt.

Bonita was beside him, her legs tucked under her, her hands resting on her brown riding skirt. "And now?" she asked quietly.

"And now you're going to get the hell out of this country. I'll find you a horse somewhere and you can clear out."

"I think not," she said.

"You think not? I think so, Bonita. You don't belong here."

"I don't belong here!" Her head came around sharply. Her moon-bright eyes flashed with emotion. "This is my country, Shelter. Over there," her finger lifted, pointing toward the promontory, a low dark mound at this distance, "that is my home. Mine! Built by my father. There I was raised, taught my lessons, there I played with my sisters, there the young men first came to court. That is my home—do not tell me where I belong."

"All right. You belong here, but right now you're going to have to give it up for a while. It's too dangerous for you to be here."

"And what will you do?" she asked, looking toward the sea which showed as a bright ribbon on the horizon.

"What do you think?"

"Fight Villa."

"That's right. Crush him."

"While I run away."

"There's a difference, Bonita," Shell began. She cut him off sharply.

"Yes, there is! The difference is that this is my fight, the fight of the people of Mexico, of Escebar, and not of Shelter Morgan. If you are here to fight with us then that

163

is appreciated. But—you will not tell the rest of us when to fight, when to run away."

"The rest of you?"

"Yes. Do you think my people are cowards?"

"You're not. I don't know how you put up with what you did."

"I had to! That is simple. You understand that, Shelter Morgan. I did what had to be done. Because there was no choice."

Shell nodded silently. He understood that all right—there were things that had to be done and a notable absence of people with the guts to do them.

"There are others?" he asked at length.

"Yes." She looked directly at him now. "Do not think the people of Escebar are cowards. But they were not willing to commit suicide, to see their children slaughtered, their town burned. They were waiting, gathering weapons, learning about Villa, because they knew if they did not fight they would remain beneath the heel of Villa forever. Who will come here from the capital? They are not threatened and so they ignore the problem. We cannot ignore it—this is our land. They are our masters. Or would be our masters, yet we will not be subdued."

It was a passionate speech and she delivered it with fire, her fine mouth grim, her eyes flashing, her entire body tense as she spoke.

"All right." Shelter grinned. "I won't send you away. I don't like it, but you can stay."

"Thank you so much," she said with some sarcasm.

"Lady," Shell said with a smile. "We're on the same side. It's just that I sort of like you. I don't want you to get hurt."

"You mean that, don't you?" she said with some surprise.

"That's right."

"You hardly know me. Really."

"I know you've got character, Bonita. Nerve and a sense of justice. You're quite a woman, and a damn fine looking one."

He had moved nearer to her as he spoke. Now his hands rested on her shoulders and her face was turned up to his. "All right," she said, her voice deep and breathy, "I'm sorry I lost my temper."

"But you're staying in this to the end."

"That's it exactly," she laughed, and Shelter kissed her. She clung to him, her body molding to his for a moment then with a sharp exhalation she pulled back, touching her hair nervously.

"Well . . ." she said shakily, "let's talk about it."

"I've never found much need for that," he said.

"Villa, I mean, Mister Morgan."

"I was afraid you did," he said wryly.

"There really isn't much time," Bonita reminded him. "In the morning Villa rides against the army garrison at Tampico. He wants the guns they have there, wants the gold payroll that will be in the headquarters safe."

"He must be crazy, attacking an army post. How in the world does he expect to get away with it?"

"Very simple—he knew that the army was preparing to transfer two-thirds of that unit to the southern states. Now, it has happened. There will be only a handful of men at the Tampico garrison. Not only that, Villa has men inside. Apparently of high rank. Once again Villa will be well armed, once again he will have money to pay

165

mercenary soldiers—and many of them. That is why we have decided we must stop him now."

"Who has decided, Bonita?"

"Myself and a man named Juan Diaz and the people of Escebar."

"Who is Diaz?"

"Just a lawyer, a man of books. His family was killed by Villa—many of us have lost family. It has gone on for long enough. If Villa steals the army gold, steals their weapons, then he will be twice as strong as ever—despite all that you have done. He must be stopped now. And so we shall stop him."

"It won't be easy."

"No."

"In fact, it's likely damned near impossible."

"You may be right, Shelter Morgan," Bonita admitted.

"But you're going to try it."

"Yes. And you—where will you be going?"

"Where do you think, woman? You're going after Villa, I'm going to be beside you and Diaz."

Again she was in his arms, and her kiss, warm with gratitude smothered his mouth.

"Let's go," Shelter growled. "If you're in such a hurry, let's get moving."

They rode toward Escebar, reaching it in the early hours. The streets were dark and empty, the horse's hoofs ringing on the stone pavement of the streets.

"To the right there," Bonita said and Shell turned up a narrow alley smelling of rotting vegetables and dogs. "Here," she whispered and Morgan halted his horse before a narrow, two-story adobe which advertised rooms for rent. That alley, the building looked as empty as every

166

place else in Escebar, but they weren't empty. Shell could feel the presence of men.

As he swung down he glanced behind him, seeing the shadowy figure at the head of the alley. Looking up he saw a head pull back from the rooftop.

He felt better now—Diaz was no fool. He had some security around. He followed Bonita to the door and she knocked. It was a minute before the door opened and by the feeble glow of a candle, Shell saw the weathered ancient face.

"You, Bonita!" the old woman said with astonishment. "Who is that with you?"

"I will explain inside, Maria. Please let us in. There is trouble behind us."

"All right." They were admitted and Shell found himself inside a dining room, empty but for them, the candlelight showing the heavy tables and chairs, the huge fireplace opposite.

"Wait here, I will bring Juan, though he needs his sleep—he was up all night talking to some soldiers from Tampico."

The old woman hobbled away, leaving the room in darkness. They stood silently waiting for five minutes then Shell saw the candle approaching again. This time it was a man who held it.

Tall, narrow, his hair wiped back, sporting a thin mustache. He was an elegant man in his way and his eyes flickered to where Shelter stood, leaning casually against the wall, his eyebrows drawing together.

Bonita crossed the room and put her arms around him. Diaz stroked her back with one hand, holding the candle with the other, his eyes still fixed on Morgan.

"What is happening, Bonita? Who is this? Why are you not at the big house?"

"All in good time, Juan," she said. "First—have you something for us to drink, something to eat?"

Juan hesitated. "I'll call Maria," he said. Then he walked to one of the long, crudely made tables and placed the candle on it. "Sit and wait for me."

He walked off to find the old woman while Bonita, with a weary sigh, seated herself. In minutes Diaz was back—he had dressed now in a worn gray suit, and in another minute the old woman was there with a quart pot of coffee, some cold meat and warm tortillas.

Shell started eating without being asked and Diaz continued to stare. "This is the American, Morgan, you told us about?" he finally said.

"Yes. He brought me out of Villa's house tonight. Things had gotten very bad, Juan."

Shelter interrupted. "Listen, there's no need to go into everything that's happened—let's talk about what we're going to do now. Villa, as I understand it, is on the march, heading for Tampico."

"Yes, but . . ."

"Tonight, Juan," Bonita Madrid said and Diaz came half out of his chair.

"So soon! But we are not half ready. Our people are scattered all over the countryside."

"Then you'd better start rounding them up," Shell said flatly. "Start rounding them up and meanwhile tell me everything you know about the Tampico garrison and the people involved."

"Yes." Diaz ran a harried hand across his face. He was brave, apparently, intelligent, an idealist, but he wasn't a soldier by profession. The planning had been his

168

specialty, whipping the locals into the proper mood. Leading them into battle—no—that was a job for someone else. "Excuse me, please. I will send Pablo and Manuel. They will ride to the outlying ranchos."

Shelter didn't answer. He was drinking the boiling coffee down as fast as his throat would work. He needed it, needed the warmth and the stimulation. His eyes felt like stones hanging from sensitive nerve endings. His body ached from heel to head and back down again, especially his leg and side where he had crashed into the tree going down the slope.

He hooked the plate over nearer to him and began eating the cold beef, the tortillas, washing it down with coffee as Bonita sat, hands clasped, looking worried and suddenly small.

When Juan Diaz returned, he told Shelter all he knew. "It is the general in command at Tampico who has turned traitor. This I have from two of his officers. They have nothing which a court martial would allow as evidence against General Telles. They would only ruin their own careers, or perhaps be killed if they tried to expose him— well, there is no time for that now anyway," Diaz said with a quick shrug.

"What does Telles want out of this?"

"An empire, Morgan. He is not so mad as Villa, but he is as power-hungry. We are used to revolution in this country. We have had many, there will be many more. The idea among senior officers is not very rare at all. This is the reason Telles is here on the east coast now—his ambitions are suspected vaguely in the higher echelons."

"But with Villa he wouldn't be king, only viceroy— unless he plans on killing Villa himself after the revolution."

"Perhaps that is it. Who knows?" Diaz said this wearily. "We are a people who want only peace and have suffered through one war after another. Now, in order to insure peace we are forced to make war ourselves."

"Sometimes," Shelter Morgan said, "that's the only way to do it."

15.

Shelter sat in the zinc tub upstairs in the Diaz house, letting the steaming water work at the knotted muscles, the strained ligaments. He had been ready to ride, but Diaz was not. He needed to await the arrival of his men; and Morgan wasn't about to go charging after Villa's army to start another one-man war. And so he waited, letting the hot water work its magic. Outside the skies were already beginning to gray. Dawn would come all too soon.

"That's enough water," Shell said as the door opened behind him. A yawning little kid barely reaching Shell's waist had been dragging bucket after bucket of water up from the downstairs kitchen.

"I thought you would have enough," Bonita said. "At least I was hoping there'd be enough to cover you."

"I'm not all that scary uncovered," Shell said, motioning with a wet hand toward the chair beside the tub. The chair where his holstered Colt was slung. Bonita settled into it, smiling.

"I wanted to talk to you," she said.

"Sure. What about?"

"Juan. He feels he must lead his men, and yet he is not that sort of man, Shelter Morgan."

"I can't convince him of that. It would be taking something away from him, his manhood."

"I know this." She smiled distantly. "I only wanted you to watch him for me, Shelter. To guide him."

"Think a lot of him, don't you?"

"Yes," she said, "I do. I think a lot of you as well," she added belatedly.

"Thanks. I think there might be a little difference in the way you think of us though."

"Maybe not so much, Shelter. But when this is over Juan will still be here, in Escebar. You, Shelter Morgan, where will you be? Not here I think."

"No."

"Juan is an intelligent man, a good man. He is a lawyer, the sort of man the people need. He would make a fine mayor, perhaps one day he will hold a higher office."

"With you behind him, the moon's the limit."

"You are nice—but do you know what I am saying?"

"Sure. Juan will be here. He's like you, he's a good man. The sort who wants to have a wife, a family, the sort who would like to move into the Rancho Madrid and put it back in shape. The kind of man who wants you—for keeps."

"If only . . ." She shook her head. "But impossible, no?"

"Impossible."

"I thought so." Her hand rested on his bare soapy thigh for a minute, then she bent low and kissed him gently. When she turned away there was a mist in her eyes. When she went out, the door slammed a little too hard.

Shelter finished up his bath and climbed out, dripping water on the hardwood floor until he reached a towel and rubbed himself down. They had left a razor, shaving soap and brush for him, and he got to work on the whiskers, ready to be rid of them finally.

There was a mirror on the wall and he dragged the chair over near it to place his gear on. Then, soaping up his face he got to work, scraping the beard away from his jaw, a familiar face slowly emerging.

He was finishing up his jawline when the second face appeared. Beside and behind his own and Morgan crouched, drawing his Colt from the holster slung on the chair beside him. He heard the shattering of glass behind his head as a bullet slammed into the mirror, splintering it to silver shards and glass dust.

By then Shell's own Colt was on its upward arc and he triggered off smoothly as it came level. The face in the window disappeared in a mask of blood as the .44 slug plowed through flesh and bone.

The door slammed open and Shelter automatically turned his gun that way, staying his finger as he saw Bonita Madrid, face white, eyes wide staring at him.

"What in the world . . . ?"

Shelter didn't answer. He walked to the window and looked out at the man sprawled on the balcony. A big man with a deep chest, a still-smoking gun in his hand.

"Is it . . . ?"

"He's a Willits. It's not Zack or Ben. I've seen both of them."

"How did he find you?"

"I don't know. He must have been a little smarter than the rest of them. He either tracked us here or he suspected something between you and Diaz."

Diaz himself had come into the room, carrying a rifle. Now he slowed his pace and walked to the window to look down at the dead man, and Shell thought he shuddered a little.

"I'll have him taken away."

"You'd also better have your people take a look around out there. A close look. I'd hate to have it happen again."

"It won't happen again, Morgan. We are ready to ride."

Shell nodded, walked to where his clothes lay and dressed as Diaz hustled Bonita out of the room. He kept his eyes on the window, knowing that Willits was dead, knowing that he would never rise up again to do harm in this world. He knew it, and yet the uncanny feeling persisted. When he had first seen the face in the mirror he had thought it was Hardy Willits, back from the swamps to take his revenge.

All foolishness, he told himself. "I'm either damned tired or getting a little old," he thought. Maybe it was a little of both.

He belted his gun on and snatched up his Winchester, making a mental note to get some more ammunition from Diaz. Then he went down to join the waiting army. It was funny, this army of Diaz's really was a people's army—as Villa's pretended to be. These people were peons, small ranchers, grocers, shoemakers, saloon-keepers who only wanted to be rid of the savage one.

And they would be. Shelter vowed that.

When he came down to the dining room he was surprised to see the mayor of Escebar there. Now he didn't look so cowardly, a bootlicker for Villa. He looked tough in a compact way and determined.

"Another pretender," the mayor said shaking Shell's hand. "Jim Pike the obedient lieutenant."

"You had me fooled."

"No more than you fooled me. It seemed expedient to

act that role. I could do more for Bonita, for the town in that way than standing up to Villa and getting myself hung."

"There's not much time for talk," Diaz interrupted. "Villa has quite a lead on us by this time."

"It's not important," Shell said. "We'll catch up with him. It might have to be after he's raided Tampico. Then he'll be more relaxed anyway, less alert."

"But others will have died in the meantime, Morgan. I think we should make an effort to overtake him."

"All right."

"And now—" Diaz looked around at the expectant faces of the citizens of Escebar. They at least had rifles, but all in all they weren't even as much of an army as the Tamaulipas. Simply because the Tamaulipas made war as a way of life. The cobbler, the bartender, the hostler hadn't had to live that way. They looked determined. Now. But what would their reaction be when the lead started flying?

"This is Shelter Morgan," Diaz was saying. "You all know me, you know I am not a soldier. This man is. He will give the commands when the time comes."

"Good." Shelter said. "Now let me give my first order—let's get going men, let's bring that bastard down by the heels."

A cheer went up and they started toward the door. Outside the dawn was breaking, orange and crimson above a slate gray sea. The gray was brought around—it had been fed and curried, and looked ready to go.

Shelter swung up, having a last glimpse of Bonita Madrid standing in the doorway, looking at her man, and then, only briefly, glancing with undefinable emotion at the tall, blue-eyed man on the gray horse.

Shelter started out down the cobbled street, his ragamuffin army behind him, and he was hoping there was some truth to the notion that right could prevail over wrong in this world, that God was on the side of the fools. They didn't yet seem to realize that by the time this day was over there were going to be empty beds in Escebar.

Most of the land to the south had been cleared of jungle. They passed small villages and farms, the people staring at them as they streamed past. Now and then Diaz would hold up to shout to the villagers, asking them if Villa has passed. The answer was always the same, extended arms, fingers pointing, a look of apprehension.

"They say he is an hour ahead of us," Diaz reported.

"Good. It's very good." At the last pueblo they had been told it was an hour and a half. They were closing on him. "He's in no hurry. Why don't we pick up the pace, Juan? Maybe we can catch up."

They did just that, lifting their horses into alternate run and canters. They didn't stop at the next tiny village to ask if Villa had passed this way—they didn't have to. There was a dust cloud pasted against the pale blue sky ahead of them and they knew they were that close.

"How far to Tampico?"

"No more than a mile. Villa must have the fort in sight now," Diaz shouted back as they rode their horses side by side down the sandy road.

"We've got him," Shelter said more to himself than Diaz. "Will the soldiers fight? Or has he got them all bought and paid for."

"Some will fight, Shelter. But there will be a war within the fort as Telles tries to arrest his junior officers."

Shell nodded. It was a chaotic situation, but it suited

176

him well enough. Villa was going to be caught between two forces, and he wasn't general enough to handle it. If he achieved the fort, all the better. The "people's army" would be trapped inside. Villa would have time to hold the gold in his hand and dream his last dream of empire, but he'd never get out again. Shelter vowed that.

They rode through a stand of trees, past an old decaying barn and suddenly they saw Tampico. There was a beautiful, sparkling bay, a river running into it, the Tamesi which flowed out of the highland jungles to merge with the Panuco before emptying into the sea. On one side of the river, the far side, was the town itself. Standing alone on the near bank was the adobe fort, and riding directly toward it, confident and menacing, was the army of the liberator, Hector Villa.

And behind that was the army of retribution with the dark angel at its head—Shelter Morgan.

Villa didn't yet seem to be aware there was anyone behind him. The idea was probably unthinkable to him, so Shelter held his people up and they withdrew into the trees to watch while Villa made his move.

"Now," the mayor said. "Now we have them—they would fall like wheat."

"Maybe. Maybe they'd do a little cropping of their own. Let's have a little patience, Mayor. You've waited a long time for this, let's not blow it now."

The wait wasn't as long as Shelter had anticipated. They sat waiting for half an hour or so, the sweat streaming off them as the day grew warm and humid, and then they saw Villa make his move.

The infantry went first, charging and yelling, firing off their weapons at no particular target. The cavalry held its position, Villa sitting among them, splendid in his scarlet

177

and gold uniform.

"Are they mad?" Diaz asked in an awed whisper.

"At least one of them is."

"To charge the fort like that—they will be cut down."

And from the ramparts guns were firing now. Shell saw men fall, heard them scream with pain, and then, incredibly, the gates to the fort swung open and Shelter knew why Villa had been so confident. Telles had done his part. The general had sold out.

Now the cavalry began its charge. Already the foot soldiers were inside the fort and gunsmoke rolled into the skies. The gunfire was staccato, at this distance like a string of firecrackers being touched off. But a hell of a lot more deadly.

"Now?" the mayor asked anxiously. The little man's face was glossed with sweat, revealing both fear and eagerness. Shelter looked around him seeing the grim, determined faces of the Mexicans, of Juan Diaz who was tense, angry.

"Now," Shelter said quietly.

16.

It wasn't all that easy to hold back Diaz's army. They could hear the guns firing, see the blood flowing, and they wanted to have a little of that action.

"Listen, we've got them trapped, don't you understand that. Do it my way and we'll have minimal casualties. Take up your positions outside the fort, down in that gully, in the trees near the river. Don't let them out of there and we've won, I promise you."

"Villa has left some men outside," Diaz said coldly. His eyes were fixed on the rear guard, perhaps thirty men who waited outside the fort while the battle raged within.

"Them," Shelter said with a grin, "you can have. Take them, Diaz. I don't have to tell you what you're fighting for."

A cheer went up again, and Morgan thought this was the cheeringest army he had every been around. Usually it was all groans and loud curses—maybe it was because these people *did* know what they were fighting for and they wanted it badly.

Peace. Freedom to live as you chose, without the clouds of fear hanging over you.

They were ready, and after making sure they knew where to take up their positions, Shelter let them go.

"Cut them down, men. Don't let those uniforms fool

you—they're no more soldiers than you are."

One of the peons lifted his voice in a blood-stirring scream, his Indio heritage rising to the surface. Shell stabbed his heels into the flanks of his gray, not wanting to be left out of this as his army surged forward, firing away from impossibly long range, their anger and excitement showing.

It was a time before the rear guard even realized that the guns were being fired not within the fort but from behind them. Several of the Villa men went down before they wheeled around in panic and started to make a battle of it.

Shell was surrounded by running horses, shrill war cries, firing guns, dust and suddenly by blood as a man near him was picked off by a Villa rifle. He screamed and fell as Shelter watched, trampled by the dozens of horses behind him.

Morgan had his rifle to his shoulder, reins in his teeth, firing methodically into the closely bunched, confused bandits. They were trying to run but there was nowhere for them to go. Shelter felt his horse shoulder one man aside, heard his scream as he touched off a shot which punched through another Villa man from shoulder to shoulder.

Still the battle was raging inside the fort itself, and part of Shelter's army surged forward, toward the open gate. Morgan rode to the point of the attack and shouted them back.

"No! Not now, take up the positions you were given!"

Diaz was yelling commands as well, and the mayor. Finally the men broke off the attack and made for their place in the woods to the east, the ditch which paralleled the road to the west.

"And now?" Diaz asked. He was wild-eyed, his hair blowing in the wind, his white shirt powder-stained.

"Now, you join them—keep command. We've got Villa where we want him. No sense letting him off the hook now. Hold your positions, cut them down when they retreat."

"Retreat?" Diaz looked toward the fort. "What if they remain inside?"

"They won't," Shelter promised.

He was smiling and Diaz suddenly realized what Morgan meant. "You're going in!"

"That's right."

"You said . . ."

"Rules don't apply to generals, Diaz. I'm going to go in and take a hand."

"Then I'm going with you. The mayor can take command."

"And get yourself killed? Not a chance. I mean for Bonita to have you in one piece when this is over."

"How can I do less than you?" Diaz asked. "Besides— I know which men we can trust, which are on our side."

"That's not important. You are. Stay out here."

"I am going with you," Diaz said firmly, quietly and Shelter nodded.

"Then, damnit," he said angrily, "let's get going. There's work to be done."

Getting to the fort was no problem. All the fire was directed at those already within, and there was plenty of firing going on. Ricochets whined everywhere like a swarm of maddened hornets. Gunsmoke lay like a pall across the parade ground.

Morgan led Diaz around to the blind corner of the fort and as the Mexican watched anxiously he slipped his saddle rope and smoothly lassoed an overhanging pole. Then he slung his saddlebags across his shoulder and started the climb up.

Morgan achieved the top of the wall and rolled up and over, staying low. Farther along the rampart he could see a dead soldier, a living one beside him firing down into the mass of men on the parade ground.

Diaz was up beside Shell, panting, keeping low as he peered over the rampart. The noise was deafening.

"Find those officers," Shelter said and Diaz, looking around blankly, nodded. He started working toward the soldier to their right. The man looked around with wild eyes, his rifle coming up, but he recognized Diaz.

"Where is Bonilla?"

"Down the line." The soldier waved to his right and got back to work. Shell, in a crouch, followed Diaz along the rampart. Below men fired from the windows of the headquarters building, from the windows of the barracks, from behind wagons, as the raiders fought their way across parade.

"Bonilla!" Diaz threw himself down next to a young captain with a lean, determined face and eyes used to commanding.

"Diaz. Who is this?"

"A friend. Shelter Morgan."

"Who's commanding these men?" Shell asked. Bonilla turned his back to the rampart and shoveled fresh loads in his ancient, brass-framed Colt.

"I am, for all the good it does. Telles is in the headquarters building with his loyal men. Perhaps twenty of them."

"Can you get all of your men to this side of the fort?" Shell asked.

"Perhaps." He nodded toward the soldier fighting beside him. Hanging from a cord around his neck was a bugle. "They would hear that above the din. But what would it gain us?"

In answer Shelter unstrapped his saddlebags and showed Diaz what it contained. All three men ducked low as a shower of bullets from below powdered the adobe wall behind their backs.

"I may not be able to get all my people out of there."

"If you don't, you stand a chance of losing them all," Shell pointed out.

"You do not have to remind me of that fact," Bonilla said stiffly. He thought about it for a minute then nodded. "All right. I don't know what else to do."

He rolled over to instruct his bugler who rose, dry-lipped and started blowing retreat at the top of his lungs. Those nearest heard the bugle and started backing toward the wall, firing as they went. Those farther away saw the movement and tried to follow, but a lot of them didn't make it. The slaughter was terrible. Soldiers were dying everywhere, the earth running with blood.

Morgan had his pistol across the rampart, firing into the mass of Villa men. He couldn't, damnit, locate Villa or the Willits brothers through the haze of smoke.

They continued to fight, laying down a barrage of lead as Bonilla's men ran toward the ramparts. Some were shot down off the pole ladders as they attempted the climb. Morgan looked down again, measuring things— those of Captain Bonilla's men who were pinned down in the barracks should be safe. The rest would have to take their chances. Villa's men were pressing toward the wall, confident of victory now.

When Bonilla nodded Shell fused three sticks of dynamite and threw them out as far as possible. Diaz was jamming fuse into more of the stuff, lighting and throwing. The first shockwaves shook the wall, heat and debris flying past. Below there was suddenly terror, horses whinnying in panic, men cursing, groaning.

It wasn't as bad as Cross Keys, Shell thought. There both sides had shelled each other with cannon for hour after hour. It wasn't as bad as that battle or several others Morgan recalled, but it was the worst he had seen as a civilian. In that enclosed area the dynamite tore them apart. Carnage and shattered equipment everywhere. The devil must have rejoiced.

"They're breaking!" Bonilla shouted and his men rose up to cut them down, working their rifles as rapidly as possible, increasing the ranks of the dead.

"After them!" Bonilla hollered.

"There's no need," Morgan said, and the captain looked at him with something near to anger until the guns from the woods, the ditch opened up and Bonilla saw the remnant of Villa's army being torn to shreds by the waiting townspeople.

Still from the headquarters building there was firing as Telles and his cornered men fought back desperately.

"We can take care of that too," Shell said. Then he grinned as he showed Bonilla three sticks of dynamite he had held out. "Right through the roof, I think."

"Come on," Bonilla said with grim eagerness.

They hot-footed it along the rampart, jumped down to a red-tile roof below and leaped a gap between buildings. Then they were there. Smack on top of the headquarters building. The roof vibrated with the gunfire from below. Shell hoped Bonilla's people on the rampart knew enough to keep their own shots way low.

184

Bonilla and Diaz began ripping tiles up and pounding away at the roof, but Morgan had a better idea. "Send someone back for my rope."

It didn't take long. By the time Shelter had the sticks fused, tied together with a strip torn from his shirttail, the soldier was there with his lariat.

"What are you going to do?" Diaz asked.

"I think I know," Bonilla said, and he rubbed his hands together in anticipation. "May I do it?"

Shell looked at the handsome, dark face of the officer, a face set with evil glee. He shrugged and handed it to Bonilla.

"Why not?"

They walked together to the edge of the roof. At a signalled command from Bonilla, the rifles along the wall fell silent. As Shell and a still-confused Diaz watched, the officer fed out the rope at the end of which the fused, lighted dynamite swung. The rifles still fired from the windows below, but it was impossible for anyone to shoot up at the roof. Maybe they never saw it coming, but if they did, it must have been the most terrifying moment imaginable.

Bonilla, his lips drawn back to reveal white, clenched teeth, jerked the rope up and outward, his eyes measuring the fuse. Then he lowered the rope a few feet and the dynamite package flipped neatly in through the window. All three men threw themselves aside, hitting the roof as the charge went off, jolting the building, sending bits of broken timber flying across the parade ground, and it seemed, lifting the roof several inches.

Bonilla sat up and stayed there, grinning widely.

"I think," he said, "the revolution is over."

It was over all right. Shelter didn't go into the headquarters building, knowing what he would see, but Diaz did and came back to throw up his guts.

Bonilla was gleeful. "There's only enough of his uniform to identify him. The rest of him is a smear on the walls."

Shelter looked up to see the townspeople coming in, gawking at the havoc the dynamite had caused. Slowly he walked across the parade ground, looking at each and every body. He found Ben Willits, every limb broken, the side of his face blown away, and then the other one.

"Bonilla! Diaz!"

The two Mexicans came to where Shell stood beside a wrecked heavy wagon. Beneath it was the man in the crushed scarlet uniform.

"He was hiding," Diaz said wonderingly. "Hector Villa was hiding beneath the wagon when the explosion flipped it on him!" That seemed to awe Diaz more than all that had gone before. Maybe he couldn't believe that a coward's heart beat beneath that exterior of cruelty and swagger. Shell could. Easily. He had seen that kind of man too often.

"He's not here," Morgan said to no one in particular. After rinsing off his face in a trough he went out, recovered his horse and started a slow search of those who lay outside the fort. He wasn't there either.

Zack Willits was gone. The man who had triggered all of this, the man Shelter had come to Mexico for. Gone. It made all the events of the hot, bloody, wearying week seem useless.

"Over." It was Diaz who said it. The young man was bursting with joy. In his eyes, perhaps, there was the shadow of unimagined horrors, but he was joyful all the same.

186

He had the right. Villa was gone. Life could go on for Juan Diaz. And everything in his future looked bright. Shell had a momentary glimpse of his own future—and it was as dark, as bloody as the past.

"We owe you. The people of Escebar owe you a great debt, Shelter," Diaz commented, interrupting his thoughts.

"Name the first son after me," Morgan answered.

"Do you think we will not?" He slapped Shell on the shoulder and moved away, his back straight, his face flushed, appearing more confident, somehow taller.

The army got the dirty job of cleaning up and the men of Escebar rode homeward, breaking into song, cheers going up as they congratulated themselves on the victory. Only Morgan rode silently, gloomily.

There was a larger celebration that night in Escebar. The buildings were ablaze with light. On the hill the Rancho Madrid was similarly lighted. There were mariachis in the street singing the happy songs, strumming their guitars, women dancing and much drinking.

Shell sat on the balcony of Diaz's restaurant, overlooking the procession in the street. He was in a tight pair of black vaquero trousers, a loose fitting white shirt puffed at the wrists, black sombrero. He sipped his wine and listened to the songs. Twice someone lifted a glass to the gringo on the balcony and a spontaneous cheer went up.

Morgan sighed and poured another glass of wine. He wasn't much of a drinking man, but this was the night for it. To celebrate, to blot out the past, to obscure the future.

He was tilted back in his chair, booted feet on the balustrade when Bonita and Juan Diaz found him.

"What are you doing here alone?" Bonita scolded.

187

"People downstairs want to see you, to drink to your health."

"It's a night for being alone," Shell answered.

"Tell him," Diaz prompted.

"Tomorrow night at the big house we will have a party to announce our betrothal. You will come of course."

"The guest of honor." Diaz said.

"No," Shell replied. "I won't be there. I wish you both the best, but I suppose I'll be moving on in the morning."

"But, why? You cannot, Shelter." Bonita took his hand between her own and looked up almost pleadingly.

"You understand, don't you, Juan?"

"Yes, I think so, Shelter. I think so. Come, Bonita, let us go down and join our guests. Our friend wishes to be alone, let us honor his request."

They went and Morgan was left to watch the lights, the swirling dancers and ponder the meaning of all of it, of his life which had become an endless war. He knew that this feeling wouldn't last long. In a day or two he would be healed, ready to ride the long trail, but just now he felt tired, empty, more than a little futile.

He had finished half the bottle of wine when his head began to nod and he knew it was time to sleep. To sleep long and deeply. And on this night, he could do that.

He placed the glass on the table, rose and taking one last deep breath of air, turned and walked down the corridor toward his room.

He swung the door open, walked in and lit the lantern. Then he went to the window and closed it, and froze. *Something* ran icy fingers up his spine and stood the hairs on his neck on end. He heard the rasping wheeze and threw himself to one side as the gun shattered the night silence and smashed the window where his head had been moments before.

Morgan hit the floor rolling and when he came up his gun was in his hand, bucking against his palm, spewing out daggers of orange flame, riddling the body of the man who lay on his bed, propped up on Morgan's own pillow.

Zack Willits fired once more even as the blood from his mouth streamed down across the bedspread, as the light in his eyes went out.

The bullet tugged at Shelter's shirt sleeve and buried itself in the wall behind him. Morgan kept on walking in. He didn't fire again, there was no need for it. Willits's gun dropped from his limp fingers and clattered on the floor. Shell could hear the sound of rushing feet outside as people pounded up the stairs.

Zack Willits was still alive, looking at Shelter with unalloyed hatred, with venom enough to poison the atmosphere around him. His mouth worked from side to side, grinding teeth together. He was trying, trying to will his body to work, to rise up and kill Morgan.

Through the blood he managed a few last, chocked words.

"I should have . . . I should have . . ."

And then he said no more. His eyes rolled back and his black heart stopped pumping. Morgan holstered his gun and said very softly, "Yea, you should have, Zack."

The door burst open and Diaz and Bonita, the others on their heels crowded in. Bonita fell back, hands to her mouth when she saw the dead man.

"Zack Willits?" Diaz asked.

"It was."

Morgan was across the room now, stuffing his gear into his saddlebags.

"You are leaving?" Diaz asked.

189

"Yes. Now I'm leaving."

"Shelter—it is all over now. Stay here, sleep. You will be safe."

"Yes, I know that."

"You have someplace you must go?"

"Yes." He kissed Bonita on the cheek and smiled at her. Then he patted Diaz's shoulder and walked through the throng of chattering, excited townspeople. He had someplace he had to go—the idea had been creeping up on him all evening.

Home. A funny sort of home, one that would have to do for a little while. He was going into the mountains to wait for Mando to heal. Then perhaps they would ride north together.

He rode slowly out of town into the empty night, the song falling away as he rode into the distance. They were happy, safe at last. Morgan had kept his pledge to the people of Escebar.

On this night he meant to take one more pledge—a warrior's pledge, and he lifted his eyes to the dark peak ahead of him, whistling as he rode toward the night-shrouded mountain and the dark-eyed woman who was there awaiting his return.

BOLT BY CORT MARTIN

#9: BADMAN'S BORDELLO (1127, $2.25)
When the women of Cheyenne cross the local hardcases to exercise their right to vote, Bolt discovers that politics makes for strange bedfellows!

#10: BAWDY HOUSE SHOWDOWN (1176, $2.25)
The best man to run the new brothel in San Francisco is Bolt. But Bolt's intimate interviews lead to a shoot-out that has the city quaking—and the girls shaking!

#11: THE LAST BORDELLO (1224, $2.25)
A working girl in Angel's camp doesn't stand a chance—unless Jared Bolt takes up arms to bring a little peace to the town . . . and discovers that the trouble is caused by a woman who used to do the same!

#12: THE HANGTOWN HARLOTS (1274, $2.25)
When the miners come to town, the local girls are used to having wild parties, but events are turning ugly . . . and murderous. Jared Bolt knows the trade of tricking better than anyone, though, and is always the first to come to a lady in need . . .

Available wherever paperbacks are sold, or order direct from the Publisher. Send cover price plus 50¢ per copy for mailing and handling to Zebra Books, 475 Park Avenue South, New York, N.Y. 10016. DO NOT SEND CASH.

THE HOTTEST SERIES IN THE WEST CONTINUES!

GUNN #14: THE BUFF RUNNERS (1093, $2.25)
Gunn runs into two hell-raising sisters caught in the middle of a buffalo hunter's feud. He hires out his sharpshooting skills—and doubles their fun!

GUNN #15: DRYGULCHED (1142, $2.25)
When Gunn agrees to look after a dying man's two lovely daughters, he finds himself having to solve a poaching problem too. And he's going to have to bring peace to the mountains—before he can get any himself!

GUNN #16: WYOMING WANTON (1196, $2.25)
Wrongly accused of murder, Gunn needs a place to lay low and plan his proof of innocence. And—when the next body turns up—pretty Mary is his only alibi. But will she lay her reputation on the line for Gunn?

GUNN #17: TUCSON TWOSOME (1236, $2.25)
Hard-ridin' Gunn finds himself dead center . . . the target of the Apaches, the Cavalry, and the luscious Tucson Twosome—and everyone wants a piece of Gunn's action!

GUNN #18: THE GOLDEN LADY (1298, $2.25)
Gunn's got a beautiful miner's daughter in front of him, and hard-case killers closing in on him from the rear. It looks like he'll be shooting in all directions!